# STONEBREAKER'S RIDGE

# STONEBREAKER'S RIDGE

## Ray Hogan

GUNSMOKE

First published in the US by Five Star

This hardback edition 2013
by AudioGO Ltd
by arrangement with
Golden West Literary Agency

ISBN 978 1 471 32087 3

**British Library Cataloguing in Publication Data available.**

Printed and bound in Great Britain by
MPG Books Group Limited

# Stonebreaker's Ridge

## A Western Story

# Chapter One

Jim Ryan rode slowly across the vast, rolling plain called the Vega. It was peaceful now; the grass was rich and green, with blue and yellow flowers clustered here and there, pines, juniper, piñon, and the tamarisk trees some folks mistakenly called tamaracks growing thickly along the sinkholes and frequently on the flats.

It hadn't always been that way, Ryan thought, his attention straying to a broad-winged hawk soaring effortlessly high overhead. There had been a time when guns flamed and the Vega was ablaze with greed and vengeance. His pa had died during those days of hatred along with several other good men.

Ryan shook his head. Best he not think of that now. There was no point looking back and remembering the past and the part his pa had played in it. Such was over and done, and like the bullet of a rifle, once fired and sent on its lethal mission, there was no calling it back or changing anything.

But he settled lower in his saddle, shoulders sloped forward, square-set face suddenly grim. Forget what once was, forget how things had been someone had counseled him— and he knew such words were true. He should forget the past, realize that now was the time for living. But somehow that thought placed a stubborn uneasiness in his mind that would not go away. Disturbed, impatient, he raked the roan again with his spurs and quickened the big gelding's pace. He had to rid himself of dark thoughts. Luckily it was not far to the Strickland place—and Ann.

Absently Ryan looked back at the towering rim known as Stonebreaker's Ridge that overshadowed the plain. A thirty-mile-long palisade, it was like a brooding, remote giant hovering over the country and its ranches. An unbroken barrier, its crest was accessible only at its far north and where it relented sufficiently to slope gently down to the town of Willow Creek. There was no such forgiveness at its southern end. There a man only by great care and labor could ascend the steep, brushy face and eventually gain the top.

Deep in thought Ryan rode on, coming finally to a halt at the edge of a shallow basin where he looked down upon the scatter of buildings that made up Tom Strickland's S-Bar Ranch. The late afternoon sun scoured the yard and corrals with savage thoroughness, pointing up their neglect and weathered bleakness. And there was for Jim Ryan a man's keen regret that such hard times should befall a once fine ranch.

But that was the way of many things. A great ranch was born in a man's high-flung dreams. By his sweat and toil it grew and flourished and became a powerful force in a land of violence, all under the guidance of a strong hand. But a day always comes when that strong hand wavers, falters uncertainly, and that dream begins to crumple and glory fade and turn commonplace. And soon there is only memory, legend to be spun around a night fire or told in the bunkhouse when day is done, and moonlight streams through the streaky windows.

That was the history of the S-Bar. In his prime there was no better man than Tom Strickland, and nothing on the west Vega, or for miles beyond, compared with the ranch he built and owned. But time eventually exacted its price, and the saddle was finally denied him. He sat for hours in his chair on the wide porch of the rambling house or out in the yard under the shade of the trees he had planted with his own hands, a man at great odds with himself, refusing to accept defeat, challenging with bristling acrimony the bitter fact that faced him: the S-Bar was finished and the bold tracks he had made across the land were fading like the trail of a drifter crossing the windswept dunes of the desert.

For Tom Strickland had been capable of all things he had visualized except one. He had no son, and for this he cursed the gods and damned the misfortune that had given him, instead, a daughter. Not that he loved her less, but in this wild and volatile land where a man carved out his share and held it by the strength of his courage, a woman had little chance. And it was not in the makeup of Strickland to lay his faith or place his trust in another man. Thus, he was at one and the same time facing the inevitable, but steadfastly refusing to admit its proximity.

Ryan stirred at seeing Ann Strickland, tall and serene, come out of a back door and strike across the yard to a pen where a dozen or more chickens scuffled expectantly in the dust. A light breeze, early for evening, plucked at her dark hair and moved it gently about her face, and he felt his pulses quicken as they always did when she was near. She emptied her pan of scraps and turned to go, and for a moment the oval of her face was uplifted toward him, but her eyes were far-seeing, and she did not notice him there.

He clucked the roan into motion and let him pick his way down the slope. She heard him coming and paused, and he saw her brush at something on her dress and straighten the white circle of collar. When he pulled up before her, she stood with hands behind her back, her smile soft and welcoming.

Very soberly he said: "Are you the lady of the house, ma'am?"

"I am," she answered, mocking his mood.

9

"Do you think you could spare a meal for a poor, hungry cowboy?"

"How hungry?"

"Well, my last meal was the tops of my old boots. 'Most anything would do."

"I'm sure we can do better than that," she said, and then laughed, unable to keep up the farce longer.

Ryan stepped down from the roan, took his hat in hand, and came near her. She waited, her face calm, her lips full and curving slightly in a smile.

He said: "Ann, you don't know how much this means to me, being invited here to supper."

"It's a small thing," she replied. "We should be better neighbors. Besides," she added after a moment, "it's pleasant having company."

"For that I thank you," Ryan said. "In six months' time I have made almost as many friends on the Vega as I have fingers on my left hand. People here are not generous with their friendship."

"I know," she said kindly. "It takes a long time, but it will come. You will see that, and you must not think them all like my father."

"I wish they were," Ryan said. "I understand him. Likely I will be just the same, someday."

She touched him with her smile, showing her appreciation. Then, as if suddenly remembering something: "I'm curious. Who are those friends on your left hand?"

Ryan shrugged. "Jules Briner, for one. My foreman, Frank Sears . . . your father . . . Ross Meldrum, perhaps."

"Four," she murmured. "No woman?"

"That is for you to answer, Ann."

"Does it need answering?" she said at once, and changed the subject. "You will find my father and George Cobb in the

10

front yard. Join them and I will bring some lemonade."

She turned for the house, and he led the roan to the corral. Tying the big horse in the shadows, he walked the short distance to the front where Tom Strickland rocked gently in his chair, beneath the deep shade of a giant cottonwood, talking with his foreman. Nodding to that man, he made his salutation to Strickland. "How're you, Tom? Looks like you might be enjoying that chair this hot day."

Strickland watched him remove his hat and wipe the sweat from his forehead and face. Ryan was lean, brown-haired, and burned dark by the prairie's constant sun. His mouth was a broad slash beneath a heavy nose, and his eyes were that indeterminate color of slate, gray at one time, cold blue at another. And for a man not yet twenty-four the smooth gravity of his features was misleading for he was a man always quick to anger and close to violence.

Strickland said: "Never gets too hot for me. As for this damned chair. . . ."

His voice trailed off, and Ryan knew he was thinking of the many things that needed to be done, the many jobs that lay unfinished. A man lived a lifetime, but never got around to doing them all. Ryan knew the feeling. There was never enough time in one day.

He said: "Anything I can do for my board?"

Strickland shook his head in an irritated manner. "Long as you're invited to sit at my table, I'll expect no work from you."

Ryan glanced at Cobb, but the old foreman was looking off toward the windbreak of a tamarisk that stretched across the north side of the yard. He was plucking absently at the straggling, yellow mustache dropping down over his mouth, his craggy profile sharp against the backdrop of green. Strickland was in a poor mood this day, and for that Ryan was sorry.

He had planned to broach again the subject of buying the S-Bar.

"You moving your lower herd to the hills soon?"

At Ryan's question, Cobb swung his gaze back from the break. He started to speak, but Strickland answered first.

"George's plannin' to do just that, come mornin'."

"Need any help . . . let me know," Ryan said to the foreman. "I'll send a couple of the boys over to work."

Strickland pricked up angrily. "I don't need none of your help," he snapped. "Not yours or Hugh Baldwin's nor anybody else's! Don't know why everybody is so all fired anxious to run my ranch for me!"

Ryan shrugged, ignoring the display of temper. A man took Tom Strickland as he found him, and Tom Strickland responded to all things according to the status of his health at that exact moment. Either he felt good or he felt bad, and his reactions to anything said or done were governed accordingly.

Cobb muttered: "Could use some help, sure enough."

"You and Dominguez can do it. Hell, man, there ain't more'n a hundred head in that bunch."

"Pretty wild," Cobb objected mildly.

"Wild!" Strickland snorted. He squirmed about in the chair, clawing at his knees. He was a small man, thin and wiry, and his eyes were black spots of sparking fire when he got worked up. "There ain't been a wild cow on this ranch in twenty years. That stuff we got's nothin' but milkin' stock when you stack 'em up against the longhorns we used to pop out of the brush around here."

"Maybe so," Cobb said in that same mild way, "but these here critters are tough to handle. I could use a rider or two."

Ann came out of the house and approached them, bringing a tray of lemonade. Ryan, roused from his leaning against the cottonwood's rough trunk, watched her, stirred deeply as he always was in her sight. Her dark hair was piled high now on her head and her face bore a faint flush from some activity she had been engaged in. She had intense green eyes, somewhat slanted, and the shape of her was set off by the persistent breeze that molded the light dress against her well-rounded figure.

"It's too hot for you to be getting excited, Papa," she said, lightly chiding him. "Maybe this will cool you off a bit."

She handed the three glasses around and, giving Ryan her smile, returned to the house.

"Hear you're buyin' up more stock," Strickland said after a time.

Ryan nodded. "Whiteman's herd. Killibrew's loaning me the money to pick them up. About two hundred head."

"Good buy?"

"Twelve dollars a head, range delivery."

"Good enough, if you're careful. What's Whiteman plannin' to do?"

"Move back to the States. Says he's got all this country he can swallow."

Strickland shook his head. "Never figured him for the stickin' kind. One of them flat-land farmers. Had no business tryin' to raise cattle. Either a man's got it in him or he ain't." He hesitated, then: "You keep on buildin' up, you'll be big as Hugh Baldwin one of these days. Or big as the S-Bar," he added in a wistful tone.

Ryan said: "Man can't stand still. Either he goes up or he goes down. There's no staying in one place."

"That's so," Strickland agreed.

"You mentioned Baldwin. He been around?"

Strickland shook his head. "Not for a week or two. Him and that flat-eyed gunslinger rode by then."

"Dan Pike's his foreman," Ryan observed with a slow grin.

"If he's a foreman, I'm a Chinaman," Strickland said. "Doubt if that one knows what end of a steer the tail hangs off of. Only thing he knows is what that Forty-Five hangin' on his leg is for."

"Two, three his boys up on the north range yesterday," Cobb broke in. "That big feller they calls Turk and Reno Davis and another one I don't know."

"What they doin' up there?" Strickland demanded, at once suspicious.

Cobb shrugged. "Just ridin', Reno said."

"Looks to me like Hugh's hirin' a right smart of new help lately," Strickland said after a thoughtful pause. "Wonder what he's got on his mind." He lifted his glance suddenly to Ryan. "Reckon you got somethin' on your mind, too, lately. You been tryin' to speak it out ever since you got here. What is it?"

Ryan smiled, his thoughts all at once out in the open. He hadn't realized it showed so plainly. It wasn't a good time to broach the subject again, but then, where Strickland was concerned, it seldom was in some matters. "I was wondering if you'd given any more thought to my offer to buy the S-Bar from you, Tom?"

He stopped, letting his eyes search Strickland's face closely, seeking the reaction to his words. The old rancher said nothing, his gaze steady on Ryan.

"Adding more stock is crowding my range a little, and I need more room and more water. I figure Killibrew would loan me enough to make a sizable down payment, and I could meet a note once a year for you, after the drive."

Strickland made no reply. He watched Ryan with smothering closeness, his shoulders coming up a little and the points of his face turning white where the skin drew down tightly. Cobb cleared his throat in the silence that fell across the yard.

14

"I wouldn't figure on you leaving the place, and I'd want George and the rest of the boys to stay on. Just add them to my crew. I'd run the herds together and make one big drive, instead of two."

Ryan stopped, having no more to say, knowing he needed more but at a loss as to what it should be. He watched Strickland lay his gnarled hands on the arms of his chair and come slowly to his feet, and he knew then he had said too much.

"You got it all figured out!"

George Cobb coughed again and got up. "Reckon I'd better wash," he murmured, and stomped across the yard to the side door of the house. The screen door banged loudly behind him.

"You and Hugh Baldwin been after my place for a long time," Strickland said between clenched teeth. "You both figure I'm on my last legs, and you can close me out. Well, let me tell you this, Ryan . . . this place ain't for sale and never will be, long as I'm alive. I know that girl of mine can't run it and couldn't, if she tried, not with you hemmin' her in on one side and Baldwin on the other. You'd wipe her out like a timber wolf runnin' through sheep."

Ryan stiffened, anger moving suddenly through him. Controlling his voice, he said: "Forget it, Tom. Forget I even mentioned it. You don't want to sell. We'll let it go at that."

"Forget it? Forget, hell! You think I don't know what you're up to?"

The unreasonableness of the man plucked at Ryan, and he tried to hold back the anger that kept pushing at him. "No need for all this, Tom. You don't mean what you've said, and I won't listen to it."

"You'll listen to what's gospel and you'll like it!"

"There's no truth in what you're saying, and you know

15

that for a fact," Ryan snapped. "I'd never do anything that would hurt Ann."

"No, nothin' except maybe swindle her out of this ranch when I'm gone!"

Ryan clung to his self-control. In a low, strained voice he said: "If anybody besides you said that, he would have to back it up. Being you, we'll let it pass."

"We'll let it pass because it's the truth. And what's more, you'll stay away from here and you'll stay away from my girl! I'll not have you around, schemin' like an Indian to lay your hands on this place!"

Still clinging to his temper, Ryan said: "I don't think you mean what you're saying, Tom. Cool off and forget the whole thing."

"Forget, nothin'! Get off my ranch, Ryan, and stay off! I don't want to see you around here again. That clear?"

Ryan, thoroughly aroused, swept the man with a glance and nodded. "It's clear," he said, and strode stiffly past him, crossing the yard to the corral. He pulled out the roan and stepped into the saddle. Coming back along the windbreak, he passed Strickland, saw him standing there rigid, his face white and contorted with his rage, his fists clenched at his sides. Nodding briefly, Ryan rode on, following the trail along the tamarisks that led, eventually, to the main road. He had been a fool to mention buying the place from Strickland. He should have known better. But when was there a better time?

Across the stillness, a gun spurt forth its sudden, shocking racket. Ryan, startled, jerked the roan to a stop. He pulled his own weapon and turned in the saddle. Tom Strickland was weaving on his feet, clutching at the spreading stain on his chest. Ann burst through the doorway and came running into the yard, her cry breaking the silence. From the side of the house George Cobb appeared.

Strickland wilted just as Ann reached him and fell heavily to the ground, and in that moment Ryan heard the rapid pound of a running horse on the far side of the tamarisk break. Throwing a glance at Strickland and seeing Cobb there now with Ann, he wheeled the roan about and drove hard for the receding sound.

Ann was conscious of Jim Ryan's pressing glance as she set the tray aside and handed the glasses out one by one to the three men. The lemonade was not as cold as she had wished, since the ice, hauled in from a lake some ten miles north that previous winter and buried deep near the barn, was about gone. But it was wet, and she reckoned that was the main thing. Having completed her hostess duties, she gave Ryan her smile and returned to the house.

Inside, she paused. She wished her father had been in a better humor for Jim's visit, but such times came seldom any more. Tom Strickland, old and crippled-up, was never in a good humor, and expecting him to be otherwise was hope-less. She could only hope that he and Jim Ryan would get along without harsh words—at least until after supper was over.

Half turning, she glanced through the window, her fingers straying to the lace edge collar of the dress she had donned es-pecially for Jim Ryan's benefit. It was her best dress, the pret-tiest one. She hoped he had noticed it. A smile parted her lips. Things appeared to be going smoothly. The three men were talking quietly while sipping their drinks.

Ann put her attention back to preparing the meal she in-tended to serve. It was a hot day, but that always seemed to make no difference to her father or any other man when it came to eating. She shook her head slightly in wonderment, perplexed as always by the contradictoriness of men. Ignoring the day's wilting heat, they would prefer a steak, fried potatoes, hot biscuits, and steaming corn on the cob, or the like, all washed down by scalding black coffee and topped off with hot, dried apple pie.

But that was the way of it throughout the Vega. It was common, everyday fare for a rancher and his family, and Ann supposed that should the time ever come when she and Jim Ryan were married, she would be preparing the same sort of meal for him.

Ann paused thoughtfully. Would she ever become the wife of Jim Ryan? She had thought of it often, even dreamed of what life would be like. She believed he felt the same toward her, but for some reason he never brought up the subject.

At first she believed she understood his reticence, that like all strong men of his kind he was possessed by a shyness around a woman and was finding it hard to bring up the matter of marriage. But as time passed and opportunities came and went, and he remained silent, Ann began to wonder. Maybe he didn't feel the same way about her as she did about him. After all, maybe he would never ask her to become his wife.

Why?

She had asked herself that question over and over. What was wrong with her? She knew she was better than average-looking, that she might even be considered beautiful when she worked at fixing up herself. Too, she could ride and handle a team, and do ranch chores right along with any man, not to mention that she was a good cook and housekeeper. Why, then, did Jim hold back?

Was her father to blame? Hard, crusty, ill-tempered, and constantly disagreeable was what other men considered him, and she had to agree. He had been that way ever since an accident that had forced him to quit the saddle and resort to a buckboard for transportation. All this Jim Ryan had seemed to understand and take into consideration. Her father was old as well as crippled and no longer could do the job he felt obliged to do, and that he had done for forty or so years, and thus his bad nature was to be expected and tolerated.

Ryan had never discussed it with her. It had just been an understanding between them. A frown puckered the tanned smoothness of her forehead, and she impatiently brushed back a wisp of stray hair. Then why didn't Jim speak up? Was it going to be up to her to do the proposing? The times were coming when her father would no longer be able to direct the running of the ranch, and it would fall squarely on her shoulders, and she would need help.

Ann was honest enough to admit that to herself. S-Bar was a giant spread on the Vega, and she was not so stupid as to believe she could, even with hired hands, keep the ranch going. She would need the strong, firm hand of a man, one who knew the business and who would not be afraid to stand up against Hugh Baldwin, who her father believed was getting ideas like his parent, Ben Baldwin, now dead, had once entertained about taking over the Vega.

Jim could do that and all else that was necessary to preserve the S-Bar and, at the same time, make her happy. She was frank to admit that fact to herself—selfish as it might be. What was keeping him back? Why . . . ?

The sudden, sharp crack of a gunshot broke the late quiet. Startled, Ann paused at what she was doing. Who could be shooting a gun so near the house? Her father had made it clear to the cowhands that such would not be tolerated. She stiffened as a horrifying thought leaped into her mind.

Whirling, she crossed to the doorway in quick steps and glanced out. Ryan was no longer there in the shade. George

Cobb, too, was gone, and her father, hands pressed to his blood-stained chest, was slipping to the ground. She saw Ryan then, mounted on his horse, gun in hand.

"Oh, no!" she cried as what appeared to be reality claimed her mind. "Not . . . not you, Jim!" she murmured as she rushed into the yard.

# Chapter Two

A man does not run a horse through a tamarisk windbreak. It is a little like being trapped, imprisoned in a bewildering labyrinth of crooked tree trunks and dangling, frothy curtains, and there are no direct passageways out. A half dozen lunges on the part of the roan, and Ryan pulled him in, fearful of the consequences, and let him pick his own course through the maze.

The break was a full hundred yards wide, as the crow flies, more by the devious route the roan was forced to follow, and, when at last they broke out into the open, the bushwhacker was little more than a boiling dust cloud in the distance. Ryan holstered his gun and touched the roan with spurs, and the big blue leaped into a stretching, ground-consuming run. They swept up the shallow valley, toward the north, keeping abreast of the buttes breaking out from the ragged bulk of the Santa Claras lying in cloud-topped silence to the east. Ryan began to gain on the escaping rider, and he strained to recognize him as the gap started to close. But the man was bent low in the saddle, and the horse he rode was indistinguishable, being either a buckskin or bay or perhaps a sorrel. In the dust he could not be sure.

While the roan hurried on, Ryan was searching his mind, wondering who the rider might be, and he was asking himself who could have hated the crusty old rancher enough to kill him. Offhand, he could think of no one. There were, of course, the usual number of disgruntled non-friends that any man accumulates in a lengthy lifetime of building up a big spread, but it was doubtful any of these would nurse thoughts of murder.

Strickland had been a stern, straight down the middle sort of man to whom black was black and white was white, and there was no room for compromise. But he had a reputation for fairness. He was never known to cheat a man (although he was a shrewd bargainer), and he never turned a hungry man from his door. In these past years when age laid its restraint upon his activities and his S-Bar began to run down, the barb of his temper sharpened even more, but he still retained the good will of all those who lived on the Vega plains and in nearby Gunstock.

The man on the buckskin, as he was now sure, appeared to be changing his plans. Ryan saw him begin to swerve, heading away from the wooded slopes and cañons of the Santa Claras in a long, swinging arc. Ryan altered the roan's course to match and, in so doing, began rapidly to lessen the intervening distance. The blue, however, immediately ran into trouble on the loose rock cropping out from the higher ground, and Ryan slackened his pace, taking no chances.

They were nearing Baldwin's Circle X south line now. Like a three-fingered hand with the heel butting up against the mountains, the ranches lay across the Vega. Farthest south was Ryan's own Box K. In the center was Tom Strickland's S-Bar, and to the north sprawled Baldwin's huge outfit, reaching out over the prairies and low hills in limitless, blue-rimmed distances. It was said of Hugh Baldwin that only he knew where Circle X began and ended. And there were those in town who thought other things, not so complimentary about the big rancher. But such words were never voiced. Gunstock was considered Baldwin's town, and a man walked on dangerous ground if he dared dissent.

Other smaller ranches spotted the country to the east and south, small, starve-out spreads that usually sold their stock to Baldwin or, at times in the past, to Strickland rather than make their own drives to the railhead beyond the Santa Claras. A half dozen winter-whipped, summer-scorched squatters fought the land on the far side of the river for a bitter livelihood, and these, plus those who lived in Gunstock proper, comprised the whole of the Vega plains.

Ryan lost ground in the rough country. He watched the rider curve into the first outreach of timber and vanish. But the roan, breaking at last from the rocky slope, leveled out again and moved in fast. Ryan reached the timber and entered slightly below that point into which the bushwhacker had disappeared, pulling to a halt well within the pines. He tried to listen, but the blue was breathing so deeply that he finally dismounted and walked ahead a dozen paces where he might hear better. It came to him then, standing there, that the rider could also have stopped just within the grove and was at that moment laying his sights upon him.

He heard nothing, and in the silence of the birds he read his answer—the man had stopped. He was close by. Drawing his gun, he walked back to the roan, the nerves in his neck prickling each step of the way. Taking up the leathers, he began a slow, careful advance, leading the roan close to him, knowing he was a much poorer target on the ground than sitting high up on the horse.

On the spongy carpet of the forest he could move quietly, and the blue's hoofs made no more than a soft *tunk-tunk*. Through the network of tree tops he could see the full blue sky, but he realized that it would not be blue for long. The afternoon sun was fading fast, and it soon would be full dark. He moved slowly on, working in and out of the junipers, the thick briers, down the lanes of pine. The deathly stillness held.

Somewhere, far up through the grove, a mockingbird

sang, and Ryan came to a stop, considering that. The sound was distant, and he came to the eventual conclusion that the bird had not been disturbed recently by anyone passing, and so he swung away, working deeper into the trees. It was then he heard the sound that again brought him up sharply. It could have been a winter-dry twig snapping under sudden weight, or it could have been a dead brush stalk giving way before a heavy body. It made him immediately alert and ready, and, as the tension built in the breathless quiet, he tried to locate the point from which the noise had come. But he was unsure, and, when it did not come again, he stepped to the saddle and sent the roan briskly dead ahead.

The grove was beginning to darken with shadows that grew steadily longer, and he was having difficulty in seeing. When nothing developed in the direction he had taken, he cut left again, rode for a dozen yards, and once more halted, straining into the half gloom for any sound. He was that way—leaning forward in the saddle, ears searching the silence, eyes probing the brush—when the gun crashed, and the bullet came reaching for him. It missed by mere inches, thudded dully into the pine near which he waited, and sent echoes rolling through the grove. Instantly he swerved the roan away and laid his answering shot at the flash of orange flame almost behind him.

He kept the roan moving, feeling better now that he had located his target. He kept circling the place where the gunman had been, snapping a quick shot into the likely points. He drove in fast from the opposite side, covering his advance with two shots. One bullet left, he reached the juniper clump where the gunman had been and pulled up. He was again alone. For a time he remained quiet, listening as before, but he heard nothing, and, neither liking his position nor the rôle of stationary target, he drifted gently forward. It was growing increasingly darker. A few minutes of light remained for the grove. The mockingbird, stilled by the blasting echoes of the guns, resumed his song, alternately trilling and challenging in his peculiar way, and then, farther on to the west, another took it up.

The roan walked into a blind alley of osage orange, and Ryan wheeled him quickly around and out, not wanting to be thus caught in a box. Once clear of that, he stopped again to listen, uneasy at the necessity, but knowing that it had to be. All advantage was with the other man, who could pause and listen to his approach. Ryan was relying almost completely upon his ears now, the darkness closing out sight a few feet from him.

There was only the roan's deep breathing and the mockingbird's song. He cut left again, moving eastward now, thinking he had lost the bushwhacker in the night. He let the roan have his own time and way, and, when he came to the edge of the grove and rode out onto the prairie, bathed now in the silvery fog of dusk, he did not urge the horse to greater speed. He was thinking of Ann Strickland and what lay before her. She would need him now, the strength he could lend her, the comfort he could give. The S-Bar would be hers to do with as she saw fit and that was the way it should be. He would see to that. If she wished to keep it, to try to run it as her own, he would help in every way he could. If she wanted to sell, he would make his bid along with Hugh Baldwin or anyone else interested, and the best price would prevail. That was the way it would be.

When the brilliant flash of the gun exploded, almost under the roan's long head it seemed, Ryan left the saddle instinctively in a long, low dive. He hit the ground on all fours, and another bullet dug sand behind him. He half crawled, half ran for the protection of a juniper clump, trying to locate the ambusher and see where he was going at one and the same time. The gun shattered the quiet again, and a bullet droned over his head. Darkness was working both ways, hiding him as it did the bushwhacker, and, when he reached the brush stand, he dropped flat and wormed his way quickly around to the opposite side.

Gun in hand, he waited for the telltale boom of the next shot, and, when it came, digging into the heart of the juniper, he snapped his quick reply. Almost in the same breath, the gunman was after him, placing his bullets, throwing sand and trash upon Ryan's prostrate shape as he searched the brush pile. Ryan rolled away, holding his fire. He came to an abrupt halt against another juniper stand and lay there, suddenly furious and exasperated at the turn of events. He could reach no advantage; he could gain no point. At each and every turn, the bushwhacker pinned him down, helpless.

Seething, he waited impatiently, trying to pierce the black face of night and locate the gunman. He was somewhere ahead, out there on the prairie, hiding behind one of the clumps of brush or lying in the protection of a low butte. He thought he saw movement and fastened his gaze upon that spot, but after a minute it all appeared to be in motion, and he shook his head to clear his vision. The time dragged by, and then he heard the distant drum of a running horse, going away from the buttes, from him, driving hard in the direction of town.

He came to his feet and started for the roan at a run. Anger still rankled through him, goading him on. The bushwhacker wasn't free yet.

# Chapter Three

Ryan reached Gunstock two hours later. He came into the north end of the street and there halted, letting his gaze run the length of the short thoroughfare. The lamps were lit, and a few people strolled in the evening's coolness, enjoying the change from the day's sharp heat. A cluster of horses stood before Jules Briner's Trailstop Saloon, patiently waiting for their riders. Sound and yellow lamplight and deep shadows and a thin haze of dust hung between the buildings in an ever-changing pattern. In this ceaselessly moving picture, he knew the killer of Tom Strickland was now hiding.

He drifted over to the rail in front of the Trailstop and closely examined the horses there. All were cold, apparently having been there for some time. Moving on through the thick dust, he rode the street's entire length to Steve Claunch's livery stable and there dismounted. The hostler came out of the building's gloomy interior and waited, flat-footed and silent.

"Take care of him," Ryan said, and handed the man the reins. "I'll be back later."

He stepped swiftly past the hostler into the stable, moving to the far side of the runway where the light from a single overhead lantern could not touch him.

"What's up?" the hostler demanded, at once suspicious. "What's goin' on?"

"Take care of that horse . . . that's all you need to know," Ryan said.

The hostler stopped talking.

Ryan drifted silently down the wide aisle of stalls. The first three were empty, but the fourth was occupied. He reached out and touched the horse's rump. It was cold. The next stall was empty, and in the remaining three he found horses, but they, too, had been there for hours.

At the end of that side he stopped, tension suddenly beginning to build along his nerves. In the nearly total darkness, rank with the strong odors of the stable, he listened, hearing the faint drops of footfalls, then a light scraping along with the vaguest rustle of cloth against the splintery rough surface of timber. Ryan stepped deeper into the shadows and drew his gun.

For a full minute he waited, trying to place the sound. It seemed to have come from the rear, from the end of the building where Claunch usually parked the buggies he maintained for hire. Staying close to the wall he walked out its length, coming finally to the first vehicle. Here he paused again to listen and probe the blackness with his eyes.

After a time he crossed the runway and made his check of the horses on that side. In the end stall he found nothing. In the next two there were horses that were warm to his touch, but likely had been in the stable for some while. He threw his glance toward the door and saw the hostler still standing there, holding the roan in close. He could not see the man's face, but he knew he was watching him.

He moved up to him and was about to place his question when the quick running of a horse behind the stable caught his attention. He wheeled and ran the building's length and out into the open. Finding himself in the wagon yard, he cut left and rushed to the alleyway. There was nothing in sight. Whoever it had been had turned off into one of the many openings and passageways and had dropped from sight. Thinking the man might come into the street, Ryan retraced his steps, but, when he reached the walk in front of Claunch's, there was no rider to be seen.

Anger and frustration again overrode Ryan. He stalked back to the hostler, grasped him by the bib of his overalls.

"Who was that?" he demanded, pulling the man up close. "Who went out the back way? Speak up, damn you, or I'll make you loose from your boots!"

The hostler's eyes spread round, and his mouth flew open. He let go of the roan, and the big blue shied off down the runway.

"Nobody . . . nobody. Wasn't nobody in here."

Ryan said: "Somebody was in here. He left when I came in, going out the back. Don't tell me I'm wrong!"

The hostler shook his head, and Ryan saw genuine fear on the man's face. He released his grip and let him fall back a step or two.

The hostler shrugged himself, settling his clothing back onto his thin frame. "Nobody here," he said. "No matter what you're thinkin', there wasn't nobody here."

Ryan searched the man's face. He could be telling the truth, he decided. He didn't know how close he had been behind the killer when he reached town; the roan traveled fast, and he could have been close. And again, the hostler could be lying to save his own skin.

Ryan said—"All right, forget it."—and turned into the street.

More lights were on now, laying their yellow squares along the boardwalks and in the dust. Keeping close to the wall of the stable, he began a slow patrol, walking softly, avoiding the bright areas where possible, his pressing glance probing the passageways between the buildings as he moved.

He reached the corner of Dunn-Jackson's General Store and halted, remembering the wagon yard at the rear of that building. He made a careful inspection of the area, finding nothing there. Returning to the street, he moved on, checking off one by one the business houses and their lots. When he reached the end of the block, he crossed over and doubled back on that side.

Killibrew's Cattlemen's Trust Bank was on the corner. Next came the two-story Kansas City Hotel, and he went carefully about that property but found no waiting horses. After that there was a row of small shops: a bakery; dressmaker; gunsmith; Coy Graham's hardware store; a saloon; and several other assorted institutions, the last of which was the combination jail and office of Marshal Ross Meldrum. The search so far had yielded nothing, and, finding himself in front of the marshal's office, the thought came to him that it would be an opportune time to bring Meldrum in on the matter. But the place was dark, and the door locked.

Ryan's anger had cooled somewhat by this time, and he took the moment to lean back against the jail, build himself a smoke, think over the past few hours, and determine his next move. A man and a woman passed by, the man nodding. He returned the salutation, hearing the broken conversation take up a yard away: ". . . the railroad in ten years."

A rider came into the street, and Ryan sharply examined the man and horse, and promptly forgot them, the man's white hat answering his question. Back in the saloon he had just passed, a piano broke into tinny clatter, and a woman laughed in a deep-throated way from an upstairs window of the Kansas City, the sound carrying far.

Somewhere in this town was the man he searched for, the man who had waited in ambush and killed Tom Strickland almost before his eyes, the man who had led him on a wild chase through the tamarisk breaks and across the prairies, into the groves that fanned out from the Santa Claras and finally back to the town. For the first time the oddity of that struck him. Why north to the groves and then double back to Gunstock? Why didn't the bushwhacker head straight for town when his job was done? It would have been much more logical.

Ryan flipped the cigarette into the street, watched its red coal glow brightly and die, then crossed over to the Trailstop, the last place to be checked. He mounted the steps and pushed through the batwing doors, the crash of sound and glare of light meeting him head on. The place was crowded, and smoke boiled along the beamed ceiling, and voices set up a steady din within the walls.

Ryan shoved his way through the crowd to the bar, seeing no one with whom he was particularly acquainted. He called for a beer, received it, and withdrew along the curving end of the bar away from the press, where he might better see those who came and went. Jules Briner moved up, cutting through the crowd from a far corner.

"'Evening, Ryan. Pleasure to see you here."

Briner was a thin, calm man, precise in manner and speech. He dressed well, lived moderately, and was unlike any saloon owner Ryan had ever known. Somewhere, sometime in his background, he had known gentility and the flavor of that lay upon him, setting him apart from the general run of those who frequented his place of business.

Ryan nodded. "You wouldn't have noticed anyone coming in during the last hour . . . in particular, I mean?"

Briner smiled and lifted his hands in a small gesture. "Be hard to say. They come and they go. I saw no one that I didn't know. You looking for somebody special?"

Ryan's hard-set features were grim. "For the man who killed Tom Strickland."

Briner waited a long minute. "Killed Tom Strickland?"

31

Ryan nodded and related the details. "I followed him into town, but he had a pretty fair start on me. I think I almost had him nailed at Steve Claunch's place, but he gave me the slip."

"You've no thoughts as to who it might be . . . you didn't get a look at him?"

"Hardly a glimpse."

Briner murmured: "A problem . . . finding him now." He voiced then the question Ryan had asked himself several times. "Who would want to kill Tom?"

"If he had any enemies, I don't know who they were."

"My guess," Briner said, "is that there is more to it than that, more than what meets the eye. Somebody had a definite purpose and reason. How's the girl taking it?"

"I didn't wait," Ryan replied. "Cobb was there, and I went after the dry-gulcher when I heard him leaving. I'll ride that way now."

"Earlier in the evening there was someone here asking for Meldrum, I heard. Likely that was Cobb."

Ryan nodded. He placed his empty glass back on the counter. "I'll drop back later. Meantime, you could check around and see if anybody has heard anything or saw anything that wasn't just right."

"I'll do that," Briner said, smiled his brief smile, and wheeled away.

Ryan turned to make use of a nearby side entrance. He paused, seeing the batwings burst suddenly inward. Ross Meldrum, closely followed by George Cobb and Reno Davis, one of Baldwin's riders, entered and came to a halt. Ryan waited, thinking to make his report to Meldrum and ask Cobb about Ann when the marshal's heavy voice broke above all other noises: "Hold it, Ryan! I want to talk to you!"

Ryan ducked his head. He settled back against the curve of the bar, little flags of danger all at once plucking at his nerves.

There was something in Meldrum's manner that was off-key, not right; the same something was in the grim set of George Cobb's hawk-like face. They pushed their way up to a point in front of him and came to a stop, fanning out, shoulder to shoulder.

Ryan said: "What's on your mind, Marshal?"

"Tom Strickland." Meldrum answered at once. "I'm arresting you for his murder!"

# Chapter Four

For a full minute Ryan stood motionless, struck wholly speech-less by the accusation. The crowd fell silent, and Jules Briner, a few steps away, halted and came slowly around, his sharp eyes searching Ryan's face. Conversation died. The tinkling of the piano ceased, and a man's rough voice silenced a woman's high-pitched laugh.

Ryan stood completely alone, physically and literally. He recognized, in those tight moments, that he was as much a stranger as he had been that day six months ago when he had ridden into Gunstock and the Vega plains country and took over the old place. His thoughts moved quickly back, and he recalled his own words, not many hours gone, when he had enumerated his friends for Ann Strickland. A ragged smile pulled at his long lips. Friends? Were these bitter-faced ac-cusers his friends?

Anger awoke and moved swiftly through him, bringing its temper close to the surface. In a tone sharp as a Bowie knife's blade, he said: "What the hell are you talking about, Meldrum?"

Ross Meldrum was a big man, thick through the body and wide across the chest. He stood a head taller than most men, and the color of his hair matched exactly the silver in his star. His broad face was square and forever flushed, as if he had been running hard, and he had a straight line for a mouth. He was a good man, an honest one, Ryan knew, and although a bit slow-witted no one ever questioned his integrity and courage.

Meldrum said: "You know what I'm talking about. Don't play cozy with me! I've got you dead to rights . . . witnesses and all."

Ryan's jaw sagged. "Witnesses? I never shot Tom Strickland. How can you have witnesses?"

"Well, I got them," Meldrum stated. He slanted a glance at Cobb. "Tell him, George. Tell him what you told me."

Strickland's foreman pulled himself erect and faced Ryan. "I saw you, Ryan, no use denyin' it. You was arguin' with Tom when I went to wash up, somethin' about your wantin' to buy the ranch. He ordered you offen the place, and I saw you get your horse and ride out. Then I heard a shot, and, when I looked, you was settin' there, gun in your hand. That's the way it was, and there ain't no use your sayin' it wasn't because I sure as hell saw you!" Cobb's eyes were snapping, his pointed chin stuck out belligerently. "Ann saw you, too," he added.

Ryan shook his head. His anger had dwindled some, and reason returned to a degree. "That's part true, but not all. Sure I had words with Tom. Who hasn't?"

"He order you off the place?" Meldrum asked.

"He did, and I left. I was invited over to eat. I mentioned to Tom again that I'd like to buy his place. He got mad about it and told me to leave."

"You sayin' you didn't shoot him, after that?" Cobb broke in.

"I didn't shoot him, George. You know that. You know that as well as you know your own name. I didn't shoot him."

"You was settin' there on that roan with your gun in your hand."

Ryan swung his gaze to the marshal. "Ross, I can straighten this out. Everything's right so far as it goes up to the point of my shooting Strickland. I left when he ordered me off the place. I rode out, taking the road along the tamarisk windbreak, but, just as I got to the end of that, I heard a shot. I stopped and pulled my gun. Tom was just starting to fall, and George and Ann were coming out to see what it was all about."

Ryan paused, seeing the doors of the saloon swing in again. Hugh Baldwin, followed by Dan Pike, came into the hushed room and stopped, surprise at the silence covering Baldwin's face. He moved in closer, Pike at his elbow like a gray shadow.

"Trouble here?" Baldwin asked, looking at Meldrum.

"Tom Strickland's been killed," the lawman replied. "Appears Ryan did the shooting."

Baldwin shifted his glance to Ryan. Once or twice before Ryan had come up against the owner of Circle X but never in anything serious. He was another big man, almost as large as Meldrum, and he took great pride in his appearance. His tastes ran to expensive broadcloths and fine woolens, and the boots and hat he was then wearing probably would pay a 'puncher's wages for a year. Ryan felt the pressure of his frankly deriding eyes and heard him say: "I figured something like this would happen. A man's ambition can ride him too hard at times. Make him do things he shouldn't."

A murmur ran through the saloon. Baldwin's words were true—just what many of them had thought. Ryan had got too big for his britches too fast. They had expected him to pull something like this one day. They should have known it would happen.

Ryan never moved his eyes from Baldwin, having his wonder at the man's definite hostility.

Meldrum's voice cut through his thoughts. "Go on, Ryan. Let's hear the rest of it."

"I heard somebody leaving on the other side of the

tamarisks. When I saw Ann and George coming to help Tom, I went after him."

"But didn't catch him, I take it."

Ryan met the marshal's disbelieving gaze coolly. He shook his head. "I didn't. He hit north and went into the hills. There was a little shooting, but he gave me the slip and doubled back into town."

"And this man that was standing in the tamarisks . . . he was the one that killed Tom?"

"It was somebody in there."

Meldrum ducked his head at Reno Davis. "That the way it happened?"

The 'puncher swaggered in a few steps, pleased at being suddenly the center of attraction.

At once Hugh Baldwin said: "What're you doing in town, Reno? You're supposed to be working the south range."

Ryan saw a quick glance pass between the two men, and then Meldrum said: "Reno's in on this, Hugh. Witness."

"Witness?" Baldwin echoed.

The marshal nodded. To Davis he said: "Go ahead, tell them how it was."

The 'puncher grinned at Ryan. "Well, like I told the law here, I was workin' the south pasture when I got a little thirsty. I was close to Strickland's place, so I dropped by for a drink, but, when I got there, I heard Ryan and the old man arguin'. I pulled up, not wantin' to bust in on a private fight, when Ryan up and shoots Strickland."

Davis paused, letting the murmur that ran through the room rise and fall. He grinned at Ryan in his wicked, toothy way while small lights of triumph danced in his eyes.

"Then what, Reno?" Meldrum prompted. "Go on . . . go on."

" 'Bout that time Ryan spotted me there, and I took off. I

figured with him in a killin' mood like he was, that was no safe place for me. Like he says, he run me clean to the hills, but, when dark come, I got away and come into town lookin' for you, Marshal."

Ryan listened to the tale with prickling scalp. The baldness of the lie appalled him for the first few moments, and then anger whipped anew through him as he realized what was taking place. Davis had killed Strickland. It had been that man, hiding in the tamarisks, who had fired the shot and then went racing away across the prairie. And now Davis was blandly twisting the truth around to where, with the few things George Cobb had seen, it appeared he had shot Strickland. But why?

He let his eyes move from Davis to Meldrum. The marshal believed the Circle X rider, that was plain. He had all the proof he needed. On Hugh Baldwin's face he saw a smug expression, a faint smile, as if he was pleased with the way of things. Ryan had a moment's wonder if that man knew more about the affair than he claimed. Had that surprise at seeing Davis in the saloon been genuine? Talk ran around the room, gradually increasing, and in this Ryan read an open threat. He would have little chance here—or later, he knew. He was being tried and convicted at that very moment.

Ryan searched the ring of faces, and those beyond, gauging their intentions, estimating their temper, and trying to calculate the next few moments. And all that time his own sharp anger was whetted into a seething sort of frustration, goading him close to reckless violence.

He said: "It's my word against that of Reno Davis. And my word means nothing to you . . . that right, Marshal?"

"His word . . . and George Cobb's and Ann Strickland's," Meldrum reminded him. "That's pretty strong evidence."

"Davis is a liar," Ryan stated in spaced, distinct words that reached every corner of the room.

"Could be the other way around, Ryan. Nobody knows much about you in these parts. You blew in with a pocketful of money and drove in a herd. And you got a hot head. That's about all we know."

Hugh Baldwin said: "Except that he's buying more cows and needs more room . . . like the Strickland place."

Ryan shrugged, an unconscious motion to stem the sudden, driving urge to reach out for Baldwin and Meldrum and all the others and bash their heads in. He let his eyes slide over the crowd and then come back to Dan Pike who was standing near Baldwin. Pike was the man to watch if he was to make a move. The little gunman's gaze was upon him, his eyes flat and empty.

Ryan came back to Meldrum. A thin smile broke his lips, and he stepped away from the bar in an easy, off-hand move. Outwardly he was cool, but within him the bright fires of anger blazed at white heat.

Meldrum said: "Come along, Ryan. I'm locking you up for the circuit judge."

With that same deceptive smile, Ryan said—"No, Marshal."—and snapped a fast shot at the lamp hanging over Meldrum's head.

The shattering of the oil lamp did not plunge the room into darkness. A dozen more kept it well-lighted, but the suddenness of the shot, the shower of glass and oil turned the crowd into a mass of scrambling, yelling confusion.

Ryan dipped, wheeled away as he fired, and lunged for the side door. He felt the breath of Pike's bullet and heard it slam into the wall behind him. Meldrum sang out his surprise, and Baldwin's voice commanded: "Stop that man!"

Ryan placed another shot into the ceiling, jerked the door wide, and plunged into the blackness of the night.

# Chapter Five

The rectangle of yellow light followed him, and he threw himself to one side, escaping it. Shouts lifted behind him, and a man appeared in the open doorway. He drove the man back with a bullet that splintered wood near his head. Behind the building he heard a horse, frightened at the gunfire, rearing and trying to break away from the rail, and he raced across the intervening distance to it. More yells were breaking into the night's solidness, and, as he jerked free the reins and swung into the saddle, he took another shot at the still open doorway. He spurred the plunging horse and rushed off down the alleyway.

A querulous voice called—"What's goin' on?"—from an upper window, but Ryan paid no heed. Men had poured out of the Trailstop's front doors and were pounding toward the alley, avoiding the side door's frame of light. A gun boomed in the blackness behind him, and he realized they had located him, yet the bullet was wide, and he knew then they had not seen but had only heard him. Faintly he caught the sound of Meldrum's booming voice shouting his instructions for the calling of a posse.

He reached the wagon yard behind Dunn-Jackson's and cut into the passageway that separated it from its adjoining building. He rode boldly out into the street, into full view, and a cry immediately went up from the front of the Trailstop. Tightly smiling his satisfaction at this, he spurred the pony to the opposite side, entered the passageway that ran between Graham's Hardware Store and a saloon, and eventually reached the alley proper that ran behind the structures on that side of Gunstock's one street. Following this, he came to stop in the shadows behind the Kansas City Hotel, and from there he watched the posse gather.

In the half darkness he could see men leading up their horses. There was a babble of talk. Meldrum stood on the porch of the saloon talking with someone, and he could see Baldwin's high shape just behind him. He stepped down and led the pony to the far corner of the hotel, pointed him due south, away from the town, and slapped him hard on the rump. The startled horse leaped away and clattered off into the night.

Almost immediately the sound of his running was heard. A man cried—"There he goes!"—and went vaulting into his saddle. Meldrum shouted something that was lost in the confusion, and then the posse got into motion.

Ryan waited no longer. He had created the diversion that would allow him to get the roan, but there was no time to lose. There was no way of knowing how far the frightened pony would lead them. He might stop soon, or the sounds of the pursuing posse could rattle him even more and cause him to lead them for miles before they would discover that he was riderless. It was a gamble Ryan had to take. He wheeled, and, staying behind the buildings in the dark alleyway, he ran the block's full length.

He came into the street on the near side of the jail and paused on the walk. The posse was out of sight, and those who had gathered to watch the proceedings were drifting back into the Trailstop and other places from which they had come. Claunch's was almost directly across from where he stood, and Ryan, fighting himself to walk casually so as to attract no undue attention, leisurely covered the distance and entered the stable.

One look at the hostler's strained face told him he had

made a mistake. The man stood under the lantern in the fan of yellow light, his eyes wide with their fear, his fingers restless.

From the darkness beyond, Hugh Baldwin's voice: "Come in, Ryan. I've been waiting."

Ryan froze, cursing his own stupidity. He should have guessed they would be watching the roan. He remained silent, watching Baldwin and Dan Pike come into the spread of light. A thin smile was upon the cattleman's lips, but Pike was a somber, still shadow.

"Never underestimate a man, Dan," Baldwin said with dry humor riding his tone. "Something I never do."

Pike had his own thoughts. He said: "Where'd you learn to draw iron like that, mister? You ever down around Fort Sumner or maybe Mesilla?"

Ryan made no reply. He was taking inventory of all things in his mind, sorting them out, searching for a way out of his present circumstances. He was now drawing his last breath, he knew, unless he did. A man like Hugh Baldwin played for keeps. The roan was still in the first stall, and this knowledge he tucked away. The hostler stood, rooted, near the wall. Baldwin was in the center of the lantern's light, and Pike was just a step aside, just within the fringe.

"Ryan," Baldwin said then, "you made a big mistake. Fact is, you made several. The first being your coming back to this country. Getting in my way was the second."

Ryan shrugged, playing for time. "Meaning what?"

"Simple arithmetic. It takes twenty acres to support one cow around here. Right now I'm running three on every acre I own. Now does that make any sense to you?"

"There's room for Circle X and nobody else . . . that what you're driving at?"

Baldwin chuckled. "You're a smart man, Ryan. I said it

42

before. I could use you. Too bad you didn't come see me at the start, instead of getting yourself all crosswise. You could have had a good job."

"Doubt if you'd have anything in my line." Ryan said dryly.

He was watching the hostler, placing his hopes on that man's throbbing fear. It showed in his eyes, in the nervous bunching of his face muscles, and in the working of his mouth. He had reached a point where the slightest unexpected thing would send him into screaming flight. In the tense stillness Ryan listened to his rapid breathing.

"Ryan," Baldwin said then, "Dan here wants to see how fast you are with that gun. You were pretty good back there in the saloon, but Dan was hindered by the crowd. Now, he's curious to know just how good you are."

Ryan nodded. He ducked his head at the hostler. "What about him?"

Baldwin said: "What about him?"

Ryan turned to the stableman. In a perfectly level, cold voice he said: "Keep out of this, or I'll kill you!"

The hostler cringed. Baldwin laughed. He drew his own gun. "What makes you think you will be in shape to kill anybody? If it turns out you're faster than Dan, I'll finish the job myself."

"And turn my body over to the marshal as a present. That the way it will be?"

"Like I said before, Ryan, you're a smart man."

Baldwin pulled away from Pike a step, coming closer to the hostler.

Pike let his hands fall to his sides, his shoulders going down, his knees breaking slightly. He said: "You never answered my question, Ryan. You from around Sumner or Mesilla? Maybe El Paso?"

"What difference does it make?" Ryan murmured.

"No difference," Pike said. "Just wondering about it."

In that fraction of time following Pike's words, Ryan made his move. In a single, blurring sweep his gun came up, and he lunged into the hostler. His bullet caught Pike fully in the chest, and that man went rocking backwards into the shadows, never getting his own gun off. Baldwin, caught by the hostler's weight, slammed into the post at the end of the stall and reeled into the runway. His gun skittered off into the dark, and Ryan closed in.

Baldwin met him with reaching hands, and Ryan dodged and sent the man stumbling back with a hard right to the head. The rancher caught himself and came back, cursing between his teeth, his eyes bright with anger. Ryan stopped him with a straight left, but Baldwin recovered and came on, swinging hard. Ryan took a vicious blow in the ribs and returned it with a crackling right that landed high on Baldwin's head.

The hostler struggled out of the way of the circling pair and moved toward the doorway. Ryan hauled him up short with: "Go through that door and I'll put a bullet in your back!" The stableman shrank back into the stall.

Baldwin suddenly rushed, and Ryan stepped to one side, and, as the man plunged on, he staggered him with two rapid blows. Baldwin recovered quickly, wheeled, and caught Ryan with his wide swinging fists, almost sending him down. A grin broke across Baldwin's face as he rushed in. Ryan backed away, pulling deeply for breath, and, as the big man came in close, he rocked him with a right to the jaw and a left that landed fully on the nose. Baldwin fell back, and Ryan pressed his advantage, following up with two more whistling blows.

Baldwin backed into the wall and staggered forward, throwing his arms around Ryan to keep from falling, and together they wrestled about the stable, locked in each other's arms, crashing into the uprights and stalls until finally Ryan broke free and stepped away. Baldwin came in after him, lashing out with knotted fists. The left drove into Ryan's ribs, throwing him off balance; the right straightened him up. Baldwin swung again, and Ryan felt the solid shock of the blow go completely through him, setting lights wheeling about his head. He hung on grimly, backing away, trying to clear his head.

He felt Baldwin's knuckles skid off his mouth as the blow fell short, but it brought the warm, salty taste of blood to his lips. His senses cleared rapidly after that, and he caught Baldwin off guard by coming suddenly to life with a stiff right to the man's belly. Baldwin stopped short, and Ryan came in fast, his arms working like pistons. Baldwin met him then, blow for blow, and for a full minute they stood toe to toe, slugging it out, filling the stable with the deep, meaty thudding of their hard blows.

Ryan plowed blindly on, heaving for breath, throwing all he could muster into each driving fist. Baldwin began to wilt, to give way. Ryan kept after him, keeping him moving under a hail of merciless fists. Baldwin's hands dropped, and Ryan brought a long, haymaking right up from the floor. It caught Baldwin on the point of his chin, half lifting him off his feet. He went backwards into a crumpled heap, crashing into the lantern post. The lantern flew from its peg and shattered against the wall.

Oil spread in a wide circle, and the fire caught with an explosive flash. Ryan, hearing in that moment the sounds of running horses outside and guessing the return of the posse, shouted to the hostler.

"Drag this man outside!"

The stableman scurried to comply. He took Baldwin by

the armpits and struggled with him toward the front door. Ryan freed his roan and fought him past the spreading flames, pointing him for the rear entrance. There were shouts rising from the street, and somebody was banging on the fire bell. He led the roan to the wagon yard at the side of the building and paused long enough to pull up the cinch. Smoke was rolling out into the night from the stable's doors and loft windows. The crackling of tinder-dry wood and the smell of burning stable trash filled the air.

Ryan swung to the saddle and wheeled into the alley. A rider loomed suddenly in the lurid glow directly before him, and he drew his gun and fired to turn the man aside. He saw then that it was Reno Davis, and he threw himself to one side on the roan as the Circle X rider's gun blossomed. He felt the sear of the bullet as it cut through his leg, but managed another shot at Davis. The 'puncher plunged away into the darkness of the alley, and Ryan spurred the blue toward the brushy hills.

# Chapter Six

In the cloud-built darkness of the night, Jim Ryan rode the blue at headlong pace. Behind him the glow of the burning stable arched over the town in a yellow-orange pall, reminding him of the rushing events that had transpired in so few minutes. And this brought bitter thought to mind. He had ridden a thousand miles and more to escape the harrying press of trouble, to escape the quarrels of men. Now, again, he was suddenly and deeply enmeshed. The past was like a relentless, pursuing shadow, never very far away, and always eventually catching up with a man. There was no such thing as a new life; the old one was never gone.

He swung the roan from the main road and struck out across the smooth, rolling prairie. He was heading straight for Stonebreaker's Ridge that lay east of his holdings, and was re-membering a lengthy run of buttes, brushy draws, and scattered piñon and juniper trees that flowed out from the base of the ridge that he and Frank Sears had ridden through a couple of times.

There was a trail that wound upwards on the flank of Stonebreaker's Ridge—an almost invisible trail off which lay several caves. If he could locate that trail, escape from his pursuers would be possible.

The roan began to tire. He had made two hard runs that afternoon with very little rest: once when they had raced after the killer of Tom Strickland, and later when they had fol-lowed him back to town. Ryan could feel the animal straining between his knees. He glanced back to see if there were any signs of the posse. It was too dark to tell, but he pulled the blue down anyway. The storm that had been in the making for the past two days had the sky covered with a lead-gray blanket. There was no starlight or moon to break it at any point.

He let the roan walk slowly for a good half hour, cooling him off gradually. Afterward he set him at an easy lope. He began then to feel the pain in his leg where Reno Davis's bullet had ripped through, and he cocked himself at an angle in the saddle, absorbing as much of the shock from the blue's motion as he could in his good leg.

It was not a bad wound. This he knew. But the sticky warmness inside his breeches leg told him it had bled considerably and was still flowing. He mulled over the advisability of stopping long enough to bind it and thus check the loss of blood, but this he ruled out. The posse could not be far behind now, even though he could neither hear nor see anything of them. And if they should suddenly appear, the roan would be in no condition for a fast, uphill run. The leg would just have to wait until he reached the safety of the bluffs.

He was on his own range. Of this he became aware when he realized he was at a point of rocks that lay a short four miles north of his ranch buildings. He was feeling a little giddy, and he had an impulse to swing down and advise Frank Sears of the night's happenings and pick up a small supply of grub and a canteen of water. And Frank could help him doctor the leg. A moment later he dismissed the idea with a shrug. That would be gambling against high odds, for Meldrum, urged by Hugh Baldwin, would send men there at the very first. They would expect him to do something like that. It would be walking straight into a cocked snare.

Anyway, Sears would guess his hiding place when he got wind of the state of things. He would fit the facts together in that wise old way of his and show up—probably before the morning. He would bring all the necessary items: food, drink, medicine—the works. A man had to move pretty damned fast to outguess old Frank.

Ryan became conscious of swaying loosely in the saddle. He caught at the horn to steady himself, shaking his head in an effort to toss off the mist that engulfed him. That hole in his leg must be worse than he had figured. The clouds floated out of his eyes, and his vision cleared. It couldn't be far to the bluffs now. He could see them, he thought, looming ahead. Great, ragged shapes of blackness deeper than the night standing in the near distance.

An owl, or some other nocturnal bird, scuttled out from the roan's feet, and the big horse shied violently. Pain stabbed through Ryan, coursing his entire body like a fiery streak. He clung to the saddle horn and tried to calm the blue with a few words. He rubbed at the horse's bowed neck muscles and patted him gently. The roan settled down once again, but the moments had brought the fog back, and for several minutes it was a struggle to stay in the leather.

The night breeze, hurrying ahead of the storm, brought some relief and refreshment. The roan had dropped to a slow walk when he was again conscious. He had reached the first gradual slopes that fell away from the bluffs. He was wishing it would rain then, knowing that it would make him feel somewhat better.

He was depending now upon Frank Sears's coming by daylight. Somehow, it had become a reality in his flagging mind, and he was not considering it would be any other way. Sears would know. He would come with grub and water. He could depend on that. Just as you could always depend upon Sears. He took a great deal of joy from being referred to as the foreman of the Box K. He wasn't actually. He had just come along with the land when Ryan's father had purchased it—same as the trees and the buildings and the ridge. Ryan had taken a liking to him, and they had been together many hours when work was light, just roaming across the property. A man would have thought the grizzled old rider was as much the owner as Ryan, so much pride did he take in the place.

"Don't need no payin'," Frank had said one day, when Ryan brought up the matter of salary.

"Twenty-five dollars a month and found," Ryan had offered.

"What'd I do with money? Got me a place to sleep and eat. And a good horse to fork. An' I ain't figurin' on goin' no place. Reckon I got about all a man needs."

"What about smokes? What about money for boots and clothes? Man needs gear now and then."

Sears had slanted a look at Ryan from beneath his bushy eyebrows. He had a way of stroking at his mustache which he wore, full and thick. "Reckon I'll just keep on moochin' what I got to have. Howsomever, I got me a ace in the hole, ever I needs one. Got a little pocket of color back there in the hills where I can always scrape me up a stake any time I need it."

"Gold? In these hills?"

"Yes, sir. Right in these here hills." The old rider had paused. He had covered Ryan with a sharp, speculative glance. "I reckon you ought to know about it bein' your property. You want to see where it is?"

Ryan had grinned. "Hell, no. You know where it is, so keep it that way. It's yours."

Frank Sears had chuckled. "Figured you'd say that. I don't make no mistakes about a man that's white all the way through. Never make no mistakes about you, child."

Yes, Frank Sears would be there. He'd figure a way to get around Baldwin's men and Meldrum's recruited deputies.

He would show by daylight, maybe even sooner. Nobody could outsmart old Frank.

The going became rougher and the roan began to stumble in the darkness, partly from exhaustion and partly from the ragged, uneven terrain. It was utterly dark in the shadow of the bluffs, a darkness that was broken only occasionally by a ragged flash of lightning, weakened by distance. Ryan realized he would have to stop and locate himself. He would have to find the draw up which a trail led. He let the roan come to a halt of his own accord and for a few minutes sat quietly in the saddle, face tipped downward as weariness and the recurring giddiness took hold of him.

After a time he roused himself, the necessity for locating the cañon with its hidden trail ceaselessly hammering at his unconscious mind. Shaking his head to clear it, he studied the irregular rim of the bluffs and the dark, broken face of the slopes lifting away from him. In the heavy night it was difficult to pick out anything of definite, familiar shape. A flash of lightning lifted the veil. Almost directly before him was an upthrusting formation of clean granite Sears had named the Thumb. That was a clue he could use. He was close to the draw, closer than he had expected to be. It would lie a short quarter mile to his left. He stirred in the saddle and turned the tired roan in that direction, allowing him to pick his own way along the shale.

The first raindrops struck him just as he reached the lip of the cañon. He was rational enough to be grateful for it. It would ease some of the fever that was harrying him, and it would serve another important purpose. There would be several good trackers in the posse, and, among Hugh Baldwin's riders, any one of whom could follow him across the prairie and up the slopes of the bluff. A good rain would wash away all signs and eliminate that possibility for him.

He wound into the draw and moved across its width, gaining the opposite side. For a half mile, he bored deeper into the slash, while the sides became increasingly steeper and the brush heavier. The steadily falling rain and the solid blackness were hampering him now, making it hard to see the faint trail, turning the slippery rocks into dangerous traps for the roan.

Well into the cañon's depth, he stopped the blue, fearing he had overshot the trail. He waited there patiently, hands clasped about the horn, shoulders slumped while rain slanted against him and soaked him through to the skin. He could do nothing until another flash of lightning came and broke the smothering darkness. His mind was not functioning too well, and this he could not understand, being unaware of how great had been the quantity of blood he had actually lost. He grew cold, and this helped some, sharpening his senses to a degree, but he could not dispel the terrible heaviness that had settled upon him.

A vivid flash of close-by lightning and the immediate crashing of thunder startled him. He saw, directly ahead, the huge boulder he was searching for. His own intuition had brought him to a halt at the right point—if only he had known it before. He urged the roan forward and worked him around the mass of granite to the narrow game trail lying there. He was on barren rock and loose shale. It was already slick from the rain and the runoff of water beginning to cascade down from the higher points. It was rough, dangerous going, and several times he hesitated, wondering if he should go on, if he should risk the roan and himself. But always he moved on. Three times in the first hundred yards the blue stumbled, almost throwing Ryan from the saddle, shooting bright flares of pain through him. But he kept on.

He gained level ground and pulled up. He dismounted.

His leg was stiff from hip to ankle, and, when he placed a slight amount of weight upon it, living fire once again poured through him. He ground his teeth and held on to consciousness. He knew he could not chance any longer the possibility of the roan falling with him. He would have to walk. Reins in hand, he started up the steep trail, bracing himself against the face of the cliff.

A sudden wave of frustration rocked through him. Damn Hugh Baldwin! Damn Pike! Damn Tom Strickland and all the rest! Look what trying to be a friend had got him! A black, wet night, struggling on the side of a bluff, a bullet through his leg. He was cold, hungry, and so tired he could scarcely breathe. Like a cornered coyote, he was scurrying for cover, looking for a place in which to hide from a marshal's posse. Worse still, a bunch of trigger-happy riders were all anxious to finish up a job on him. Why did it have to happen just as he was getting things under way?

Limping badly, Ryan gained the second level break. He paused there to rest, leaning heavily against the roan. The trail that he followed worked along a bench about halfway up the side of a cliff. It was, perhaps, six feet back from the edge. Scrub oak and twisted juniper and dove weed growing thickly in that intervening space screened it from the prairie lying far below. In places it was fairly wide, but generally it was narrow, and, as they moved slowly along, there was a steady scraping noise as the roan's sides rubbed against the cliff's rough surface on one hand, the thick growth of brush on the other.

The rain had stopped. He realized this, standing there against the blue, hanging onto the saddle horn while he supported his weight on his good leg. He rested out another minute or two, and then, taking up the reins once more, he resumed the ascent. In the first dozen yards he stumbled twice and would have fallen flat had he not been clinging to the blue. But he managed to keep going, and finally he had completed the last half mile to the third leveling where there was the cave he sought.

There he dropped to his knees, not totally unconscious but filled with an exhaustion so vast it had no beginning, no end. Even breathing was an inhuman effort, and it seemed hardly worthwhile. But the tremendous vitality and determination of the man were such that they would not let him stop until he reached complete safety. He struggled to his feet and drove the roan back from the trail, deeper into the flat. A scatter of ghostly-looking trees lay in a small group to the rear, and into this he sent the blue. There he could not be seen, should any of the posse or Circle X riders happen to come up the trail.

After that he half walked, half crawled to the cave that was, in actuality, a low-roofed, tunnel-like crevice at the base of a cliff hinging at right angles from the main formation. Water had drained in and stood in shallow pools on the floor, but that went unnoticed. The relief in just being off his feet, clear of the trail, and out of sight was like the fulfillment of a wonderful dream.

He lay there for a full hour or more, eyes closed, senses dulled to the pain throbbing insistently through him. Weariness, a powerful anesthetic in these moments, was an ally. But the nagging pressure of necessity would not let him rest for long, and after a time he roused long enough to bind the wound crudely with a makeshift bandage.

He did not again lie down. The natural weariness of Ryan prompted him to place himself in a sitting position against the cave's back wall, facing the opening. In this way, gun in hand, he settled down to wait for Frank Sears.

# Chapter Seven

Ryan came awake with the sun's first warming rays. He was lying prone, having tipped sideways sometime during the night. He was cold, and his leg throbbed dully, but the faintness was gone, and now he was only weak and hungry.

He pulled himself to the mouth of the cave, where the sun's rays were beginning to strike, and looked out. The roan was cropping grass in the grove, and the sky was an overbending canopy of clearest blue. He could not see the prairie from the crevice, and for a long time he just sat there slumped against the rough, scaly wall, gathering heat and strength. Finally, feeling up to it, he crawled through the opening. It was perhaps thirty feet to the edge of the bench, but he had to see what was happening on the prairie below, and he went the entire distance on his hands and knees, favoring the injured leg all the way.

Parting the tangled growth of shrubbery, he lay flat and gazed out upon the rolling world below. It fell away from the base of the cliffs in yellow-gold waves, like a sea just before sunset. The night's rain still lay upon it, and the streaming sunlight caught up the bright sparkle and capped it all with a silvery sheen. It was a beautiful world, a land he had dreamed of one day becoming a part of—and now, instead, he was an outsider. He murmured under his breath, cursing the fates that had twisted all things around him. A man sometimes thought he owned his own soul, that he was captain of his own life. How quickly he learned otherwise!

He turned his eyes southward and saw the faint smudge of

buildings that marked his own Box X Ranch. He saw riders, too—an even dozen of them, spread out in a wide, slowly moving dragnet, working toward the north. More men were there, crawling like torpid ants toward the hills. He could not see it, but beyond that group lay the Strickland place. He wondered, then, which group was Baldwin's and which represented Ross Meldrum's posse. It made no particular difference, but he concluded, finally, that the larger group in the south, coming from the Box K, was the marshal's. And that would be Hugh Baldwin and his Circle X crew to the north.

They were sweeping the country for him; they were methodically working toward a central point, converging, attempting to pocket him and trap him between their two forces. They knew he had headed due east when he left Gunstock, and they knew, also, about how far he could have traveled since they had been close behind. They knew he was there, hiding somewhere between them on the prairie or in the hills, and they were moving in for the kill, driving him into a squeeze, catching him between the opposing jaws of their human vise. He smiled grimly. They would be damned surprised when they found their vise empty.

For a good hour he lay watching. The sun climbed steadily, and, as is the way of the high plains country, he began to feel the bite of the lifting heat. In this land a man was a toy of the elements. At night he shivered and froze under the touch of the mountain breezes sweeping down from the peaks and ridges. In the day, the sun drove him mercilessly, sucking his body dry and cracking his lips and creating an ever-present urgency for water. He shifted to his side, letting the heat drill into his injured leg.

Insects began to clack in the brush, and deer flies darted about and settled upon him with irritating frequency. He ripped a fan of oak leaves from a nearby scrub and brushed at them to keep them moving. Five yards away in the trail, a gray squirrel came to sudden attention, watching him with beady black eyes and scolding with sharp severity. The roan ate steadily on, with his teeth making loud, grinding noises. Occasionally a stirrup became fouled in the shrubbery, and he would pull impatiently away, throwing his head high, as if irritated by the obstruction.

Eventually tired of watching the slowly moving figures still far off on the prairie, hungry and becoming increasingly stiff, he crawled back to the cave. Despite his condition he was still a careful man, and he paused every few feet to wipe away the tracks he left behind with the oak leaf fan he had saved. He doubted if any of Baldwin's men or the posse members would ever find the hidden trail up the cañon's wall, but he took no chances, the old inbred caution in him having its way.

The cave, which earlier was cold and damp, was now a cool and comfortable haven from the sun. He lay back full-length, unmindful of the hard, rock-studded ground. The leg was a constant ache, and there was now a stiffness in his knee. But he was not too uncomfortable. Given a little more rest, some food—particularly coffee—and a decent dressing of the wound, he would be in pretty fair shape again. He had been hurt worse before. Maybe he hadn't lost quite so much blood, but there had been worse injuries than this hole through the meaty part of his leg. It was the stiffness that worried him most. Sooner or later he would have to come down off the bluffs, and that would not be easy if he were unable to make good use of the leg. Walking or riding, it would be rough going.

By noon he had given up hopes of Frank Sears's coming, but that was understandable. With the prairie below crawling with men searching every square foot of it for him, Sears would take no chances of leading them to him. He would take no risk of being seen. But Sears would come eventually. Ryan was still convinced of that.

Around the middle of the afternoon he crawled back to the rim of the cliff again. The two groups had finally met and now, together, were working out the draws at the foot of the bluffs. Brush was thick in that area, and it appeared to be slow work. When he saw two riders turn into the cañon from which the hidden trail curled up, he dragged his way tediously back to the cave, again wiping out his tracks. Inside, he once more settled himself against the wall, drew his gun, and began a lonely vigil.

But by dark no one had come up the trail, and hunger was now an insistent factor within him. He crawled to the cave's mouth and considered his best move. Hunched there, staring into the star-studded wall beyond the bench, he heard the faint click of metal against stone. A moment later there was the distinctive creak of leather as a man shifted in the saddle. Ryan pulled back into the cave and waited, gun ready, eyes boring into the darkness.

A rider swung around the turn and came into dim view. Man and horse were briefly silhouetted against the sky, and Ryan lifted his gun, ready to press off a certain shot. He thought there was something familiar about the man and his mount, but he could not be sure, and of that he had to be. He waited while the rider eased in closer.

"Jim? You 'round hyar?" Frank Sears's voice called softly.

A sigh gushed from Ryan's lips. "In here, Frank," he said, and lay back against the cave's wall. It had been a long, tough day, but, finally, it was about to end.

He heard Sears walk his horse back into the grove where the roan grazed and then return, his boots making small, hollow sounds on the hard surface, despite the care he was taking. The old 'puncher came into the cave dragging a sugar sack behind him. He holed up in a corner, squatting on his heels Indian-fashion.

"Figured you'd be here. How long?"

"Since last night," Ryan answered. "Got anything to eat in that sack?"

"Sure enough," Sears said. "Thought you might be needin' a nip of this here firewater, too. Nothin' like firewater to heat up a man's innards."

Ryan shifted about and took the bottle. He pulled the cork and tipped down a long swallow. The liquor raced down his throat like a hot stream and had an immediate effect. He shook his head, wondering a little at the shock.

Sears said: "Reckon we better have a middlin' fire in here." He moved out into the open, gathered an armful of dry wood, and returned. He cracked some of it into short lengths and laid them in a pile. "You sure got the whole dang' country out lookin' for you, son."

Ryan grinned into the darkness. The whiskey was stirring his blood to a boil, driving the chill from his bones and muscles. His stomach, so long empty of food, was reacting quickly. "Looked like a pretty good fire there in town, judging from what I could see of it," he said.

Sears chuckled. He struck a match with a thumbnail and held it to the pile of wood. After a moment the flame caught and began to twist up through the darkness, creating a warm flare of light.

"Set there in the openin'," Sears directed. "Don't think nobody's goin' to spot the glow, but there's no use takin' any chance."

Ryan moved to comply, working his stiff leg like a pivot. When he was in the cave's mouth and settled, he glanced up and caught Sears's sharp eyes studying him.

"You hurt? They wing you?"

"In the leg. Nothing serious. Got a little stiff on me, just lying around on it."

Sears snorted. "Why the hell didn't you say somethin' about it?" He set aside the can of water he was about to place in the fire and swung around.

Ryan said: "Never mind it now. Few more minutes won't make any difference in the leg. But I don't think I can last much longer without a cup of coffee!"

Sears chuckled and turned back to the fire. He started the water, adding more fuel to the flames. From the sugar sack he produced some hard biscuits, jerked beef, dried peaches, a tin of tomatoes, and a jar of ground coffee. The water began to simmer and then boil, and he dropped a generous handful of grounds into the can and set it aside. When it boiled up, he stirred the froth down with a twig. Then wrapping the can with his bandanna, he handed it to Ryan.

"I reckon you'll find it hot enough," he observed laconically, "and probably strong enough to peel bark offen a pine tree."

Ryan sipped the scalding brew, burning his lips, the inside of his mouth, and thoroughly searing his throat. But it was good, and after two or three swallows he already felt much better. He began to eat, then, making a meal of the jerky and other items. He finished it off with a long drink from Sears's canteen of water.

"Now, let's see about that there leg," Sears said, having waited patiently for Ryan to eat. He tossed more wood on the fire. "You lay down here where I can see better."

Ryan stretched out on the cave's floor. Except for the dull aching in his leg, he felt good now. The liquor, aided and abetted by the steaming coffee and food, had poured new life into him. Now, with his belly full, things did not seem so bad, after all. He had seen worse times, very much worse, he reflected.

"Goin' to have to cut your pants leg a bit," Sears stated. "It's stuck to the place where that bullet went in."

He dumped the remainder of the coffee and refilled the can with clean water. He placed that back in the fire to heat, noting: "You sure did do a right smart lot of bleedin'. A good thing, too, I'd say."

"I knew I was losing a lot of blood," Ryan answered. "Made me a little wobbly for a time." He waited a moment, then: "You been at the ranch?"

"All day."

"Meldrum and his posse stop by there?"

"Bright and early lookin' for you. He left a couple of Hugh's rannies to watch for you."

"Who? I know them?"

"Reckon you do. One's Pete Santee, other 'n' is Al Thompson."

"Have any trouble giving them the slip?"

"Nope," Sears said laconically.

"What did Meldrum have to say?"

"What'd he say? Only that you shot and killed Dan Pike after him and Baldwin cornered you, and that you knocked Hugh flat and set fire to the stable, tryin' to kill him off, too."

Ryan felt Sears working with the point of his knife around the wound, cutting free the patch of cloth that had dried hard with blood against the injury. He winced a little when Sears laid a steaming hot pad on it.

"Not quite the way it happened," he said after a moment or two. "I dropped Pike. He forced me into a draw, and I beat him to it. Baldwin and me then got into it, and during the fight the lantern came off the peg and started the fire. The hostler will tell that."

61

Sears wagged his head. "You ain't figurin' on him standin' up for you, are you? Not against Hugh Baldwin." He applied a freshly heated pad to Ryan's leg, stroking gently across the wound, saying: "What's this business about Tom Strickland? What happened there?"

While the old 'puncher worked at the injury in his leg, Ryan related the incidents of the day, concluding with the fight at the stable and the brush with Reno Davis. Sears listened, clucking periodically like a mother hen tending a lone chick. When Ryan was finished, he said: "Just about what I figured. Reckon Hugh's findin' it mighty hard to swallow your pushin' his outfit around this way. There any whiskey left in that bottle?"

Ryan handed it to him.

Sears said: "You think it sure enough was Reno that bushwhacked old Tom?"

"Can't see how it could have been anybody else," Ryan replied. In that next instant he almost yelled out when Sears poured the raw whiskey into the bullet hole.

"Need us a bandage now," Sears said, tossing the bottle into a corner. "You'll be hoppin' around good as new, before long."

"I wonder," Ryan muttered. "That kind of doctoring could wind up with 'most any sort of results."

Sears grinned. Ryan swore softly, still feeling the fire seeping in deeper. But he knew the leg was better, despite the violence of the treatment.

"Now you wait a minute while I go fetch a blanket," Sears said. "I'll rig you a pallet here alongside the fire. You keep that leg good and warm all night and it'll be limber like, come the mornin'."

# Chapter Eight

Later, after Ryan had laid himself full-length and as close to the fire as possible so the heat might soak generously into his leg, Sears said: "How long you plannin' to hole up here?"

"Not too long. Somebody will finally find this place. They'll keep on looking down below until they've checked every possible place, and, when I don't turn up, they'll start working up the sides of the hills. Could be I'll make a try for it tomorrow."

Sears wagged his head. "Too soon. Men are as thick as flies on spoilt beef, combin' out the draws and flats with a fine-tooth comb. Even saw a couple back up on the bluffs, clear on top. You better wait out tomorrow and make your move the next day. Some of them waddies'll peter out before then and go home, and you'll have a better chance. Besides, that leg of yourn needs another day's rest."

"Expect you're right," Ryan agreed after a moment. The thought of men searching along the row of the buttes disturbed him. "What about the riders you saw up above? There any way down to this ledge from there?"

"Never did find any," Sears answered slowly. "Only trail along this bluff I know of is the one you followed up here. And it quits about a quarter mile on. I don't think you need to be worryin' none about them seeing you. Just be careful they don't spot you when you get out on the trail."

"When I leave," Ryan said, "it will be in the dark."

Sears refilled the improvised coffee pot and set it back into the fire. "Reckon I could use a cup of coffee before I take out, seein' as how I probably won't make the ranch much before mornin'," he said. "You might leave what's left of that grub. Never know when me or you might have to come hustlin' back."

Ryan nodded. Changing the subject, he asked the question that had been bothering him. "Frank, what was the trouble between Tom Strickland and Baldwin? I'm dead certain it was more than Tom just not wanting to sell out to him."

Sears added a handful of sticks to the fire. It blazed up brightly, and, with a longer branch, he nestled the can of water deeper into the flames. "You're right. That sure wasn't all of it. There was just a lot of little things that grew into big ones."

Ryan built himself a smoke and handed the sack of makings to Sears. The tobacco was still a little damp from the rain, and he had some difficulty in getting it lit. "That's the way it goes most of the time. Things that don't amount to anything, someday can cause a man to slap his leather. Well, old Tom was a cantankerous old mossy horn, anyway. When he was younger, he was a tough one, but not much ever riled him unless'n it was rustlers and the like. Howsomever, after he got older and all stove up, he was sure somethin' to be sidin'. I worked one day for him a couple years ago in July, cuttin' and brandin,' and, by granny's nose, I'd starve before I'd ever do it again! Never saw such a man! Everything I did was wrong! Didn't make no difference what I had a mind to do, he was ag'in' it. Never saw so danged much contention."

Ryan reached into the fire for a burning branch with which to light his cigarette. Outside, a slight wind had arisen, riffling swiftly through the brush and along the face of the cliff, setting up a soft sighing in the tree tops. "How did he and Hugh get so crossways?"

Sears finished preparing the coffee and set it to one side to settle. "Reckon that started about five, six years ago. Hugh had a pretty fair bunch of cows on that south range of his'n, and it seems they drifted down into Strickland's herd. That crowded things a mite, and, when Tom found them, he had his boys drive them back up on Circle X graze and told Hugh about it.

"Next week or so he found that same bunch of stock down there again, right in the same place. He just rode right over to Hugh and ordered him to send some of his crew down and get them, and durn quick! Well, Hugh did that, actin' all the time like it was a big joke and he was doin' it just to humor old Tom. But, turned out, it wasn't so funny later.

"Next time Tom found them critters on his land, he didn't say nothin' about it to Hugh. He gathered up his boys, and they drove all Baldwin's stock they could find eighteen miles down the creek and into the brakes."

Sears paused. He took up the can of coffee and drank deeply, sighing his satisfaction. For a time afterwards he sat quiet, eyes staring into the fire, an old-timer remembering events that pleased him. A half smile was on his mouth, and the glow from the flickering flames touching his straggling mustache and whiskery face turned him a deep bronze.

"Baldwin do anything about that?"

"He sent his crew down after them. Took them two weeks, as I recollect, to pop them critters out of the brush and get them home. But Hugh never opened his mouth to Tom about it. Just let on like nothin' happened. But he sure didn't steal no more graze from Strickland!

"Then, one day, Tom and some of his crew went up to bring in the stock that had been summerin' in the high country to drive them down into the valley for winter. Well, they couldn't get within a country mile of any of them.

George Cobb told me later he'd never run across such a crazy bunch of critters in all his life. And knowin' George, that's coverin' a heap of territory."

"Really spooked," Ryan murmured. "Some of Baldwin's doing?"

"Who else? George said he found out them Circle X boys had done everything from hazin' them with knotted rawhide to spittin' tobacco juice in their eyes. Ever' time they spotted a man on a horse, they'd take off like a scalded pig, and they wouldn't quit runnin' till they was clean out of sight! I saw that herd after they finally got them in, and I never laid eyes on such a poorly bunch of cows in all my life. And comin' from down in the south Texas, I've seen some poorly ones."

"Strickland?"

"Why, he acted just like Hugh did. Didn't say nothin'. Just went right on like it was nothin' unusual for a man to have a plumb loony herd. But the thing had really started there. From that time on they wasn't on no more than bare speakin' terms. They'd pass not more'n twenty feet apart and make out like they didn't see each other. That ended the sparkin' Hugh and Tom's gal had been doin', too."

Ryan glanced up. "Hugh and Ann? Didn't know there had ever been anything between them."

Sears's eyes twinkled. He gave Ryan an indulgent, understanding smile. "Don't reckon it ever amounted to much. Mostly Hugh's idea, I think. But that sure cooked it, anyhow."

Sears glanced at the cold cigarette butt held between his fingers and then tossed it into the fire. "The next year, I think it was, a bunch of Strickland's cows got in with a couple of Baldwin's bulls. Later, when Tom found it out, he rounded up a dozen calves at brandin' time and drove them over to where the Circle X bunch was workin'. All he said to Hugh was . . . 'Here's the calves I owe you.' . . . and then rode off, proud and stiff-backed as you please.

"After Tom had quit his ridin', he got worse, and things between him and Baldwin really went to hell. I don't know if he thought Hugh was pullin' anything on him or not, but he sure did act like it. And when a man's settin' and wonderin' and suspectin' things and can't get around to find out nothin' for sure, either way, I guess it's the worst kind of thinkin'. Somethin' that just gnaws and chews on a man's vitals till he's danged nigh crazy. I know old Tom was about that way."

Ryan shook his head. "Not many things worse," he murmured.

"Winterin' stock got to be more of a problem for Baldwin," Sears continued. "And he finally swallered his pride and rode over to see Tom about buyin' that north section of his ranch. Tom wouldn't even listen to him . . . wouldn't even let him talk. He got real stirred up and accused Hugh of about everything you could think of, includin' a little rustlin'. Naturally, Hugh didn't take kindly to that kind of talk, and he got mad and cussed old Tom to a fare-you-well. And that's the way it's been ridin' ever since."

Ryan shifted his position on the blanket. The fire was hot, and he could detect the faintly scorched odor of cloth too near the flames. The throbbing had left his leg, and it felt some better. "Not much there for one man to shoot another over, but it's been done for less."

"You don't think that's much reason? If you knew Hugh Baldwin better, you'd be wonderin' what stalled him off long as he was. Anybody gets in Hugh's way gets tromped, once he makes up his mind to do somethin'. That Circle X outfit is big, and gettin' bigger. Hugh needs more grazin', and I reckon he's decided to get it."

"What do you figure he'll do about the Strickland place now?"

"He'll get it, that's what. Sure as water's wet. It's that north section that lays along his line that he needs bad, but that won't keep him from takin' it all if it works out that way. Could be, if he got that strip, it'd pacify him, but I sure wouldn't take no bets on it. It's like Hugh, now that he's made his move, to go whole hog and pull up only after he's got everythin' that's took his fancy. He'll figure he's settin' in a game with a pat hand now, since there's only Strickland's gal left at the S-Bar."

"You think he'll just try and move right in on her and take over the place?"

Sears shook his head. "Not this time . . . not where the gal is concerned. He'll first try to sweet talk her into sellin' out the place to him, and then, if she won't see it that way, things will start happenin' around the ranch. And they won't be good things. Sooner or later, she'll have to sell."

"You seen her?"

Sears leveled a glance across the fire's glow. "Nope. But from what I've been hearin' around the posse, she ain't thinkin' kindly thoughts about you. Hugh's got her sold that you killed her pa."

"She knows better than that," Ryan murmured.

"Well, if she does, she sure ain't actin' like it."

"Somebody ought to warn her about Baldwin."

"Way Hugh's got it fixed, I don't think she'd do much listenin', 'specially from you."

"Well, she may have to before this is over."

Sears remained silent for a time, having his own thoughts about the matter. "Reckon I'd better be moseyin' along. Man can't afford to push his luck too far."

He crawled to the cave's opening. He stopped there, thinking of something, and turned around. "Now, I don't want you worryin' none about your place. Me and the boys will take care of the old Box K. And stay off that leg for another day."

Ryan stared into the fire. "Been wondering . . . did Hugh's pa get along with Strickland?"

"Nope, he sure didn't. Old Ben Baldwin had big ideas about takin' over the Vega . . . same as I figure Hugh has got. That was the cause of all the hell around here when you was just a youngster . . . Ben a-tryin' to do just that. Was during that ruckus your pa got shot up and danged nigh went under. He was one of the ranchers with guts enough to strap on their iron and stop old Ben cold."

"Pa never mentioned any of that to me, even after I'd grown up some," Ryan said and shrugged. "Fact is, he never talked much about anything."

Sears grinned. "Old Hiram sure wasn't much for talkin' . . . I'll agree to that."

Ryan nodded. "My thanks for coming, Frank. Watch yourself going back . . . no use of you getting caught up in my troubles."

The old 'puncher snorted. "I can take care of myself . . . don't fret none about that. As for Hugh Baldwin, I'd miss a meal of fried chicken and a woman's biscuits to aggravate that man a little."

Ryan watched him squeeze through the opening and disappear into the darkness of the night. Minutes later he heard him pass by, leading his pony, as he headed down the trail.

# Chapter Nine

Sometime around midnight Ryan awakened. The fire was down to feebly glowing embers, and it was bitterly cold inside the cave. He scratched around and found a few sticks of the wood Sears had brought in and tossed them onto the coals. After a bit of fanning with his hat, he brought the flames to life. Pulling the blanket up over his shoulders, he built himself a smoke and sat there, a hunched, somber shape gathering in the scant warmness the fire was throwing out.

He was thinking of Frank Sears's words. And the more he considered them, the more disturbed he became. Hugh Baldwin, in true form and character, was now established in his mind, and he had him, at last, pegged for what he was—an utterly ruthless, wholly selfish egotist. Ryan's past experience with men of his caliber recognized that fact. A man gets big, and the feeling of power possesses him and takes over his life, and from then on it is like a runaway fever, never letting him rest, never letting him call a halt. He tries his hand and comes out on top, and from that moment on he is lost. Everything he sets his will to get, he does, by one way or another, the kinds of ways never mattering much. And those who happen to fall in the line of action suffer the consequences.

But eventually somebody comes along that does not frighten so easily, that fails to back down when things get rough. A little man, perhaps a man that's lost everything and doesn't give a hoot because there's nothing more to lose and not much farther to go. Or possibly a drifter with an urge to right the wrongs of the world and become a hero in a land

70

where heroes are short-lived. Or maybe a man who was just plain sick of seeing big men push little men around, of seeing the Hugh Baldwins rush in like wolves when the gates are open and the lambs unprotected. *Like me,* Ryan thought, startled by the realization.

For a time he let that mull about in his mind. It bothered him, and he tried to shake it off, but it remained there, firmly anchored, and his thoughts were suddenly desperate. *Maybe I am that man. But I don't want any of it. I don't want any of this fight. I've had all the gunsmoke I want in this lifetime, and I'm through with it for good.*

He shrugged and tossed the burned-down cigarette into the fire. Something became clear to him, and a deep sigh moved gustily through his wide lips as he recognized another truth. *I'll never be through with it now, if I stay here. I'll never find that peace I'm looking for on the Vega. Hugh Baldwin's put his mark on me, and now it's fight or run—and I'm through with fighting. I got into this thing by accident. I'll get out of it the best way I can, and the quickest.*

He felt of his leg, rubbing it carefully and testing its sensitivity by gentle prods and squeezes. It was still sore but not as stiff as it had been. Frank Sears's treatment and the fire's warmth had done wonders for it.

Still thinking of Baldwin, he left the cave, remembering Sears's instructions not to put his weight on the injured leg just yet, and crawled to the edge of the bench. The sky was a dark, star-studded bowl overhead, and the prairie a silvery sprinkled mist far below. Tiny spots of orange fire marked the camps of the posse members and the Circle X men posted at intervals, like a sparkling band across the Vega plains.

They were waiting for him. They knew he was there, hiding somewhere in the maze of draws and cañons and brush piles. And when morning came with its bright, revealing light, they would again begin their search. And eventually they would find him. No man could hide forever.

Seeing the winking campfires brought the old days washing back through Ryan like a rushing flash flood. Men on the hunt. Men on the dodge. It was always like that, and there was never any end to it. When one stopped another began, and a man could spend his life in the doing of it if, somewhere along the line, he did not call a halt to it. And Jim Ryan had called that halt one bloody day in the dusty street of Tascosa. But now it could begin all over again.

He came to a standing position, gingerly trying his weight on the weakened leg. It began to ache immediately, and he paused, waiting to see if it would become worse, the pain more intense. When it did not, but remained merely a dull throb, he took a few tentative steps, and, finding those not too bad, he walked back the distance to the cave. By the time he reached there, he had come to a decision. He would not wait out another day; he would not hang on until the next night to leave the hills. He would go now, while the blackness of the night still held. If Frank Sears could get by the posse and Baldwin's men, so, also, could he.

Before putting out the fire in the cave, he tore the blanket Sears had brought into narrow strips. Looping them over one arm, he took up the canteen of water and walked to the roan. He moved slowly and carefully, placing no undue strain on his bad leg, endeavoring to avoid any objects in his path that might cause him to trip or stumble. Sears had removed the blue's bridle and loosened the saddle cinch and put the horse on picket. He remained quiet while Ryan got him ready for riding.

Sears had not mentioned it, but he had not believed any of the posse would be camped within the cañon. More than likely they were out in the open where they could more easily watch the brush along the foothills and see a man if he tried to break out onto the prairie. Gambling on this being fact, Ryan tucked the strips of wool into his saddlebags and swung, stiff-legged, onto the roan. It required several minutes to find a comfortable position, but he finally managed it. He turned then toward the trail.

It was slow going but not too difficult. Starshine made the narrow trail fairly distinct, and the roan was a sure-footed animal that took his own sweet time when the going was tough. The only bad moments in the entire descent came when they were along the narrowest part, and the roan, hugging the cliff's wall, dragged Ryan's leg against the solid, rough surface. It swept his breath away when the pain stabbed through him, and he knew the bleeding undoubtedly had started again. But there was nothing he could do about it.

At the bottom, he halted in the deep shadows, well off the trail. If he had been heard coming down, there would be someone along to investigate shortly. He drew his gun and waited quietly, but after thirty minutes had dragged by he came to the conclusion that the occasional *clink* of the roan's shoes against stone and the scraping noises his infrequent contact with the cliff's face had made apparently had passed unnoticed.

Now was the time for care. He took the strips of blanket from his saddlebags and bound the blue's hoofs, folding the wool several times to deaden completely all sound. The roan did not like it much, but after a few experimental steps he decided it was all right, and forgot about it. Ryan, gun in hand, swung back to the saddle and began the long, slow ride out of the cañon.

It seemed better to follow the trail. It was open and no brush dragged against him, setting up that loud, cracking noise. There were no sounds from the blue's hooded feet, and

Ryan strained to keep the creak of leather to a minimum by doing no shifting about and maintaining a slow, regular pace. In the pale, eerie light, they drifted silently along like ghostly shadows.

Ryan saw the glow of the campfire before he reached the end of the draw. It was a good fifty yards out. Two figures lay near the smoldering coals, heads pillowed upon saddles, sleeping restlessly in the night's chill. A third man hunched close by, arms doubled across his knees, head resting face down. They were evidently alternating at watch, and this one was finding the long, quiet hours hard to fight.

Just within the shadows, Ryan studied the situation. Farther left, a hundred yards or so away, another fire flickered in the darkness. The same distance to the left lay a similar camp. In each, a guard was visible against the low flare of light. Others, if there were others, were lying beyond the fire's range and were not to be seen. Far back on the ridge, a coyote suddenly threw his challenge, shrill and lonely, into the night, setting up a string of faint echoes that laughed through the cañons and hollows. The man on watch stirred uncomfortably, but he did not lift his head.

Ryan waited out a long five minutes. Then, touching the roan lightly, he moved gently left, following out the sandy bed of the narrow draw. He struck a course that would take him approximately halfway between the two camps, a strip that was somewhat darker and more shadowed than any other and where any noises made by the blue would be least likely heard.

He was well out in the open country when the guard woke. Ryan, realizing instantly that motion, even in the solid blackness, could be detected, pulled to a quick halt. His nerves pinching a little, he watched the man as he got to his feet, stretched, and yawned noisily. He spent a few moments rubbing his face and neck and ears, endeavoring apparently to drive the sharp chill from them. Afterward, he bent down and gathered up an armful of wood and tossed it onto the fire. At first there was only an answering billow of smoke, but he poked around for a time, and finally a burst of flames broke into the night. Satisfied, he then drew a sack of tobacco from his shirt pocket and leisurely built himself a cigarette, taking great pains in doing so. This finished, he glanced about the camp, throwing his eyes into the encircling night, but the fire lay between Ryan and the guard, and he knew the man could not see him.

It was a long ten minutes. Holding entirely still in the saddle and keeping the roan from making any sound-lifting movements were nerve-wracking chores. And despite the coolness, beads of sweat formed on Ryan's brow. He was ready, his plans laid, if the man discovered him. At the first sign, he would place two or three bullets not at the guard, but into the fire. This would create no little confusion and give him time to get the roan under way at top speed. It would be tough on the bad leg, but he would just have to endure that. And whether he could lose the posse and Baldwin's men, who would come storming in at the first shots, was problematical. But at least he would have a good chance.

The coyote yipped his wailing lament again into the night, and the guard listened, cocking his head to one side. But eventually he settled back down, having had his smoke and stretch. The fire once more was burning strong and its spread of warmth was lulling him into a state of drowsiness. Ryan breathed deeper. He waited until he was sure the guard would not rouse again, and then put the blue back into his slow walk. His leg was bothering him some now; perhaps it was the strain of the moment, or it could be the after-effect of having been dragged roughly against the cliff when they came down the trail, but he ignored it. He knew the bleeding had stopped, and that reassurance helped.

He maintained the slow pace for a full mile until the camp-fires were but tiny spots in the far night. The roan was anxious to be let out, to run in the sharp coolness, but Ryan kept him in check, taking no chances. When they reached a shallow bowl that dropped below the plane of the prairie, he pulled up and came slowly from the saddle. Taking his knife, he cut the strips of wool from the blue's hoofs. They would not be needed now, and they would hamper the roan's speed if left on.

Once again in the saddle he swung due south, and just before dawn spread long fingers of light out from the east, he halted in the tangle of cedars that edged out from the hills bordering his ranch. The ride had been a cold one and had brought a steady throb in his leg. He sat, half-cocked around in the saddle, favoring the wounded leg in an awkward, stiff position.

From where he rested, he could see the back of the buildings that made up the Box K. In the gray half light, they seemed to be forlorn and deserted.

# Chapter Ten

Ryan came off the roan stiffly, settling his weight slowly upon his good leg. Sears had been right. He should not be using it, should be giving it more time to heal. To have waited another day would have been better. But a great urgency was driving Jim Ryan. He wished he could get out of this country and its quarrel. He knew only too well the chain of action and reaction that would come now as a result of Hugh Baldwin's moves. He had tasted his share of that way of life before, and he wanted no more of it. He wanted to get away from it before it pulled him any deeper into the blood-soaked mire.

Something was wrong. It was too quiet, too empty looking around the place. No smoke was coming from the kitchen flue, and this was far from being right. The cook should be preparing breakfast for Sears and the crew long before this hour. And there were other things that did not appear as they should: no horses were in the corral, except Sears's little pony, when there would have been several all saddled and bridled, ready for the day's work. No sounds were coming from the barn, no talk, no laughter, no creak of leather or heavy noises from livestock moving about.

Dark suspicion closed in upon Ryan. He glanced sharply at the bunkhouse, a short distance to his left, while a river of tension and worry began to flow through him. If any of the crew were around, most likely they would be in there. Sears had said two guards had been posted on the ranch, but he could see no sign of them. However, they could be in the main house and their horses tied to the rail in front of that building. From where he stood he could not see that point.

Ryan looped the blue's reins through a short juniper. Doubling back for a short distance, he limped silently across the open yard at its narrowest, keeping a close watch on the closed doors and drawn shades of the main house. He reached the bunkhouse, noting the back window was open. Removing his wide hat, he stepped up close and laid a cautious glance into the room. It appeared empty. The usual piles of gear were missing from the corners, the coat and hat pegs stripped.

The odor of tobacco smoke struck his nostrils, and he swiveled his search to the bunks lining the near wall. Frank Sears was lying flat on his back in one of the lower beds. His fingers were laced across his belly, and he was watching smoke drift upwards from the cigarette clamped between his lips, strike the slats overhead, and curl back in small, boiling clouds. Ryan checked the room once more. Sears was alone.

In a loud whisper he called: "Frank!"

Sears rolled swiftly to his feet and faced the window. He threw one startled look at Ryan and waved him toward the door. "Hurry it up. Them jaspers'll see you."

Ryan moved as fast as possible to the front of the building. Sears held back the door, and Ryan brushed through, favoring the leg by bracing himself against the wall with his left hand. Sears closed the door and dropped the bar across it.

He said: "They spot your hide-out?"

Ryan settled himself on the edge of a bunk. He shook his head. "No point in staying there. What's wrong here? Where's the crew?"

Sears ignored the question. "You know, you ain't showin' much sense runnin' around on that leg while it's still pretty raw. You ought to stay off it another day."

"It'll be all right. I said . . . where's the crew?"

Sears met his gaze straight on. "Gone. Every danged one of them. Run like skeered rabbits."

Ryan was not too surprised. No man could be blamed for refusing to set in a game where the odds were piled up like they were here. He said: "Baldwin come here?"

"Not that I know of, but them two rannies are still in the house waitin' for you to come back. I understand they did some pretty strong convincin' with the crew. They had all gone when I got back."

Ryan moved to the window and looked toward the main house. It was still closed and silent. He could see the two horses now, waiting hipshot at the rail.

In a wondering tone Sears asked: "You figure they really expect you to come back here? That you'd be that crazy a danged fool?"

Ryan half smiled. "I'm here. Looks like maybe they're right." He shrugged. "Hugh covers all the possibilities." Ryan went over to a bunk and sat down. "How come you didn't pull out?"

"Me? I don't scare so easy. Figure I got just as much sand as they got. I've spit in the eye of better men than them two sleepin' over there on your bed. They took my gun and told me to stay put here in the bunkhouse. They're tryin' to make a cook out of me," the old 'puncher added, with a show of distaste. He walked then to the window, as Ryan had done, and for a time let his glance rest upon the yard. Turning about after a moment, he said: "They's a lot of places you could have gone to hide out. Why the hell did you come here? I told you they was watchin' this place."

Ryan shook his head. "They're watching everywhere, Frank." He lifted his gaze to the old 'puncher. "Doesn't make any difference, anyway. I'm getting out. I want none of this fight."

Sears stared at him. A long, falling—"Ahhh."—slipped from his lips.

"I'm in this thing deeper now than I thought I would ever let myself get. I know this kind of trouble, and I'm sick of it. I came here to get away from it, not get right back in the middle of more of it. I'll not be dragged into it any deeper. They can have it 'cause I'm pulling out now."

"Knowin' you, I can believe your reasons," Sears observed slowly, "but I don't figure that's goin' to satisfy the others and what they'll be thinkin'."

"A long time ago," Ryan answered, "I quit worrying about what other people think. Man has to live with himself and that's who he's got to stay right with."

Sears nodded his understanding. "But what you goin' to do about this place? You got every dime you had sunk into it. You just ain't goin' to walk off and leave it, are you?"

Ryan shook his head. "No, that's one of the reasons I came here. I want to ask a favor of you. Killibrew at the bank told me he'd buy any time I wanted to sell. I'd like for you to see him and tell him that the time has come. Tell him I'll take that standing offer of his and to just handle the sale and hold the money for me. I'll get in touch with him later."

"You can figure on Killibrew doin' you right," Sears murmured absently. "Howsomever, there's goin' to be a right smart lot of people around here sorry to hear about this."

"How do you figure that?"

"Good many thought somebody'd finally moved into this country with enough backbone to stand up against Hugh Baldwin and his Circle X Ranch. Reckon they're goin' to be plumb disappointed now."

"They are the ones that let Baldwin and Circle X get big," Ryan said, a little stiffness riding his voice. "He wasn't always the big shucks he is now. When he started showing the signs,

80

that's when they should have pulled him down to size."

"You're sure right," Sears agreed readily, "but fact is . . . gunpowder needs a spark to set it off. That's what they been needin' all this time, somebody to be the spark."

Ryan let his gaze run through the open window to the slowly lightening day outside. "I'm not that man," he said wearily. "I've had my time at that. Let them get somebody else. There's plenty of men around."

"What about Meldrum? He's still got you pegged for killin' Tom Strickland and Dan Pike. When you turn up missin', he's goin' to spread the word in all directions."

"He'll find out who killed Tom," Ryan said. "And Dan Pike went down in a fair and even draw. The hostler will testify to that."

Sears snorted. "Supposin' Meldrum ain't got the sense to figure all that out. Or the hostler won't speak up. Then what?"

Ryan shrugged. "I'll be a long way from here, Frank."

Sears wagged his head. "Well, I can see you're set on driftin' along. Maybe you're right. I don't know. Smart men don't mix in other people's fights. I was sort of figurin' it the other way, though . . . like this is your fight and not somebody else's. But you ought to be knowin' best about that. Now, what about that stuff of yours there in the house? You want to go in now and get it? I suspect you and me could handle them two waddies in there, without much workin'."

Ryan grinned. "I suspect we could," he said, the old rider's belligerent confidence bristling all over him. "But there's nothing in there I need. Anything Killibrew don't want in the sale is yours."

"Nothin' in there I'd want," Sears said, "unless, maybe, I could have them shirts."

"Shirts?"

"Them fancy duds you got over at San Antone that time and then didn't like."

Ryan said: "I told you a long time ago they were yours if you wanted them. I thought you had them by now."

"Just never got around to it, I reckon," Sears murmured. "I'm obliged to you. When you plannin' to leave?"

"Now. One thing I've got to do first, though. I owe it to Tom Strickland to see Ann and warn her about Baldwin. And I'd like to talk to her and convince her I had nothing to do with Tom's shooting."

"You got yourself a right big chore," Sears said, pulling at his mustache. "How you goin' to get there without bein' spotted? 'Specially in broad daylight. Those hills and flats are crawlin' with men."

"Figured to drop down to the creek and ride up through the brakes. Don't think they're looking for me down there yet."

"Been one or two along there," Sears said. "But most of them are still back along the bluffs. You might get through if you keep your eyes peeled and your ears open." He walked to the window and glanced to the main house. "First, we got to get you away from here without bein' seen."

Ryan came to his feet. "Somebody out there?"

Sears said: "No, but they're inside, and up and movin' around by now. Here's what you do. I'll go in and stir them up a mess of breakfast. When they set down to eat it, I'll give you a high sign and you get out of here quick. Savvy?"

Ryan nodded. "I'll swing down through the lower meadow. They can't see that from the house."

Sears moved for the door. Reaching there, he paused and half turned. "You sure you want it this way? You're throwin' away somethin' mighty nice. If you stick around, I figure there'll be a lot of good men line up with you to see this thing

82

through. And you can count on me, all the way."

Ryan said: "Frank, there's no place worth what this is all going to finally cost." He smiled and extended his hand to the old 'puncher. "Thanks for saying that, anyway. I'll wait for your sign."

Sears grasped Ryan's hand. "All right, son," he said. "Good luck."

# Chapter Eleven

Frank Sears, returning from town and the visit to Killibrew at the bank Jim had asked him to make, led his pony until he reached the point where he knew he could turn off the main trail. Angling through the brush and low, green trees, he moved along the route he knew so well from years of working the Box K, keeping to the dips and hollows and avoiding being silhouetted as often as possible. When he was briefly exposed on a short flat, he came to a point where he dismounted. Bending low, he walked beside his mount presenting the appearance of a riderless, stray horse wandering across the Vega plains.

It was a part of the great prairie that held a particular attraction for Frank Sears. Grassy, gently rolling flats, it was a distance from the buttes but in the shadow of the stern, dominating, and unchanging presence of towering Stonebreaker's Ridge. Somehow when there he always was imbued with a sense of freedom from the world and an aloofness toward the men who dared desecrate such a beautiful country.

This excluded Jim Ryan, of course. Jim, like his pa, Hiram, was a square-shooter and a man you'd be proud to ride the river with. He wished now he had told Jim that a time back, when he was in town, he had got a paper made out that willed the gold mine to him. Frank reckoned it wasn't much, but, if Jim ever decided to quit ranching, the mine would carry him along for quite a spell. Maybe now it would have helped persuade Jim to stay and see this thing through.

A short time later Sears reached the edge of the swale in which the buildings of the Box K lay, and halted. Then, taking no special care, he rode boldly on in and slanted to the upper corral. Dismounting, Sears tied his horse to the rail and angled across the hardpack to the main house.

Al Thompson's crackling voice immediately challenged him.

"Where the hell have you been? Where'd you sneak off to?"

Sears's thin shoulders stirred indifferently. He had never had much to do with Thompson or the other Circle X rider, Pete Santee, who had been left to watch for Jim Ryan, but recent events had crystallized a mild dislike into a decided hatred. "Didn't sneak off. Hell, man, this is a workin' ranch. I got things to do."

"Like what . . . maybe rakin' out the barn?"

One of the stray dogs that had taken up residence near the bunkhouse began to bark furiously. Sears listened for a few moments, and then spat into the nearby fireplace.

"Nope. Just happens there's a little jag of cows grazing down on the east range. Been there for quite a spell. Went down there and started them drifting towards a water hole. Critters ain't got sense enough to look out for themselves."

Thompson cast a glance at Santee. "You figure this ol' bastard's telling us for true, Pete? I sure don't trust him much."

"Reckon I don't either," Santee replied, drawing a well-burnt, corn-cob pipe from a side pocket and knocking the ashes out on a nearby table, "but he's here now. Can't see as he's done no damage . . . anyways, we still got him."

Thompson rubbed at the back of his sunburned neck, doubt showing plainly on his weathered face. "Now where you think you're a-goin'," he demanded as Sears started across the room. "You for sure you didn't see nobody while you was out pushin' them cows?"

The old 'puncher grinned, shook his head. "Sure enough seen a couple of jackrabbits and a coyote, but we didn't do no talkin'."

"You're a real smart aleck, too, ain't you," Thompson snapped, his ruddy face growing even more red with anger. "I'm talkin' about men . . . like maybe this here Ryan that we're waitin' for."

"He ain't likely to show up around here," Sears said with a shrug.

Santee laughed. He was a short, dark man with thick shoulders. "Was just a-thinkin' some of them jackrabbits I've seen around here are big enough to saddle and ride. Maybe, if we'd go. . . ."

"Ain't nothin' funny about this, Pete!" Thompson cut in. "Baldwin said we . . . now where the hell you think you're goin'?" he broke off as Sears started across the room. "I've got a feeling he ain't telling us the truth. How about that, old man? You for sure you didn't see Ryan out there?"

"When I went to move them cows? Nope, sure didn't," Sears answered, and continued across the room.

"Maybe he's got Ryan hid out around here somewheres," Pete Santee suggested. "Like up on the ridge or off in that thick brush below here. What about that, you old horn toad, you got your boss stashed out to where ain't nobody can find him?"

Sears grinned. "Now, I can't rightly say, but I don't recollect nothin' like that." He hesitated and wiped at his chin with the back of a hand. "No, sir, sure can't," he added, and continued toward a short hallway just off the kitchen.

Thompson came to quick attention, his tall, lean shape stiffening as he whipped out his gun. "Where the hell you think you're goin'?"

Sears halted before a closet door and opened it. Reaching

in, he brought out several shirts. "Just getting somethin' Jim Ryan gave me. Been forgetting to take them over to my bunk," the old 'puncher said, holding up the three garments for Thompson to see. "Mighty fancy, ain't they?"

Thompson grumbled an answer of some sort, and then, as Sears turned for the door, he drew up once again. "Now where do you think you're goin'?"

"Over to the bunkhouse," Sears replied. "Aim to stash these here shirts in my warbag so's I won't be forgetting them again. Now is that all right with you, Mister Thompson?" he added, voice thick with sarcasm.

Thompson's features hardened. "Go ahead, but just you don't try running off again."

"You're the ramrod around here," Sears responded and, passing through the doorway, headed across the open yard for the crew's quarters.

Thompson spun to face Pete Santee. His rough features were again flushed, and his eyes were bright. "That old bastard sure gets under my skin, but I reckon I can sure fix that," he snarled and, taking up the rifle leaning against the wall nearby, stepped up to the doorway.

# Chapter Twelve

In the willows and dogwood along the creek, it was shaded and cool. Ryan, needing rest from the saddle even after so brief a ride, pulled the roan to a halt and came gently off the blue's wide back. He rested himself against a young cottonwood and let the big horse have his drink of the cold and clear water. Afterwards, he led him into a stand of tall brush and there, perfectly screened, turned him to graze and stretched out full-length on the damp grass.

He had lain there but a short time when his ears caught the muted *tunk-tunk* of a walking horse. He realized immediately that he had been followed. The roan paused in his cropping, and he lifted his head toward the back trail expectantly, but after a brief time he resumed his eating. Ryan cautiously pulled himself to a sitting position. The sound of the approaching horse grew louder. Ryan, gun now in hand, calmly waited out the long moments.

It was Turk Paulson, one of Baldwin's riders. He was a huge beast of a man—powerful, dull-witted, and with a single-purpose mind that resolved itself into one straight and narrow groove: hate anything not Hugh Baldwin's. Ryan saw him come in close to a thick stand of willows, saw him throw his hard, suspicious glance in a wide-reaching circle. The man knew Ryan was somewhere near, but not seeing him checked him, brought him to a halt. He had little reasoning power, this Turk Paulson, and, now faced with something he could not see or touch, he was at a standstill.

Knowing this, Ryan kept entirely still, obeying that first

law of nature that not to move is not to be seen. He watched Turk's shaggy head pivot slowly on its bull-like neck, searching through the shadows and other likely places where a man might hide. When his eyes came to the willows where Ryan and the roan were, they halted. Ryan prayed the blue would not choose that moment to move.

But the big roan moved. He lifted his head, ears cocked forward, and stared expectantly at Paulson's horse. Paulson emitted a triumphant snort. There was a creak of leather as the man shifted hurriedly in the saddle. There came a crash of brush, and Ryan knew the Circle X rider was rushing him.

He came to his feet, pain wrenching through the wounded leg as it took more than its share of the sudden motion. Disregarding it, he stepped into the saddle and spun the roan about to face Paulson's charge. His gun was in his hand, but he was reluctant to use it unless it became an absolute necessity. Paulson would not be alone. There would be others working along the river, and a gunshot would bring them piling down upon him.

He sent the roan out of the willow stand in a broad leap, almost colliding head on with Paulson. The big man yelled—"Hey! What the hell you doin'?"—in a startled, surprised voice and jerked his horse savagely away.

The roan hit the ground and stumbled momentarily in a tangle of half-exposed roots. Paulson, fighting his horse, swung back and drove in close. He crowded up alongside the blue, reaching for Ryan with a huge hand of outstretched fingers. Ryan ducked and struck out with the barrel of his gun.

Paulson slid from the saddle, hitting the ground on one heel and going on over backwards. A sort of amazed look lay across his dark face. But in a matter of seconds he was back up, shaking his head like some wild, furious animal, and coming in again. At all costs, Ryan knew he must keep clear of those reaching hands.

The roan was with him in that thought. The threat of those outstretched arms and crooking claws was a mutual fear, and, as Paulson came crashing in, the blue backed nervously away in a tight, narrow circle.

"Whoa! Whoa!" Paulson roared.

The roan wheeled away. Ryan held the gun poised, looking for another opportunity to use it. It came almost at once. The roan, pivoting blindly, came up against a stand of briar. He recoiled from the sharp thorns, and Paulson, caught suddenly and helpless to check his own forward motion, plowed into the blue's front quarters. Ryan brought the heavy six-gun down hard. It landed squarely on top of the man's head. Paulson hesitated, his eyes clouding. A pained expression crossed his face, and he began to weave a little uncertainly. Ryan brought the pistol down once more, and Paulson's knees buckled. He fell away, going down like a sack of grain ripped open.

Ryan did not wait to see if the man would rise. He straightened out the yawing roan and put him forward at a fast walk, striking north. Strickland's place would be the last place they would look for him now, and they wouldn't expect him to be going in that direction. Once on S-Bar land he could feel reasonably safe.

But getting there was something else. More men must be along the creek. He would have to look sharp. But he covered three miles before he saw another man. Ryan did not recognize him, but he gave him a wide berth, taking no chances. He wanted no more engagements such as he had just experienced with Turk Paulson. The exertion had reopened his leg wound, and he could feel it bleeding heavily again. Frank Sears's bandage was doing a good job of holding it in check, but you couldn't expect it to stop it entirely under such circumstances as the last few minutes had provided.

He cursed softly. It was sheer bad luck that had put him in line with Reno Davis's snap shot. An inch more and it would have been a clean miss. On the other hand, an inch the other way and it would have been far more serious. He would not be out on the roan as he presently was. He would either be holed up, unable to get around at all, or he would be in Ross Meldrum's hands, roosting in the jail, or, finally, he would be dead.

When he came to the bridge that lay near the Strickland place, he stopped. The buildings, lying a short quarter mile away, looked remote and deserted. The shades were drawn, and the doors were closed. There were no horses that he could see in the corrals, and there was none standing at the rail. In front of the main house he recognized Ann's pony and buckboard.

He did not move directly across the open ground, but rode on northward for another mile, waiting for a time when he would be sure he was not being followed. Then he loped the short distance to the tamarisk windbreak that had sheltered Tom Strickland's killer. Again cautious, he pulled up and waited. No one was coming from any direction, it appeared, and he drifted deeper into the tamarisks, working closer to the house.

He left the roan standing within the windbreak at a point close to the house and moved quickly to the front door. Trying the knob, Ryan turned it and pushed open the door and stepped inside. The room was cool, dark, and empty. He crossed it, heading for another door that led into the kitchen. It was slightly ajar. He moved silently through it, coming to a stop just inside, leaning against the frame to rest his leg. Ann was sitting quietly at the oilcloth-covered table. She was turned, partly away from him, her hands folded in her lap, her eyes lost in something beyond the open window. She was thinking of her father, he knew.

Some slight noise he made caused her to turn instantly. She came up from her chair and wheeled to face him, the surprise in her eyes turning to swift anger.

"You . . . you . . . !"

"Don't be afraid," Ryan said, a slight twist of sarcasm in his voice. "I'm not here to hurt you."

He felt the close, searching scrutiny of her gaze. He saw her pause at the blood-spotted area on his breeches and at the bandage showing through the hole Sears had cut. "You've been hurt!"

Ryan smiled. "Nothing serious."

"They said you were hiding in the hills. What are you doing down here? What do you want?"

She was cool now, in perfect control of herself and her emotions. She seemed drawn, a bit pale, the last few days having taken much out of her.

Ryan said: "Two things. I want you to understand and believe that I had nothing to do with the death of your father. I'm truly sorry about it, Ann."

She met his gaze steadily, her face a pale, serious oval beneath the wealth of dark hair. "You said two reasons."

"You can't stay here alone, now."

The expression on her face did not alter. "You expect me to believe anything you tell me? I saw you there, on your horse, your gun still in your hand. Reno Davis saw you shoot. Why should I doubt what I saw myself?"

"Because it's not the way it happened. Reno Davis shot your father." He paused. Then: "Ann, look at me. You know I couldn't do a thing like that. I couldn't pull a gun on your father, must less shoot him down."

She faltered momentarily. "I . . . I didn't think you . . . ,"

92

she said, breaking a little. But immediately she regained her composure. "The marshal says the proof is all there, that there's no question about it."

"The marshal is an easy man to convince, particularly if Baldwin's got anything to do with it." Ryan shifted his weight, leaning more heavily against the door frame.

"What else was it you wanted?" she asked then. "It was something about me not being safe here."

Ryan nodded. "Hugh Baldwin's on the move now to take over this range for himself. He won't stop at anything. You can't stay here, Ann. Not until it's all over. It will be too dangerous."

"What makes you think Hugh is going to do this? Did he tell you?"

Ryan said: "Of course not. But I know his kind. I've been up against them before. I know how the Hugh Baldwins do things in this world once they get the fever. Believe me, Ann, you can't stay here and try to stand against him."

"Believe you?" she echoed, her voice lifting. "Why should I believe anything from you? A gunman, a killer that shot down one man and tried to kill another. A man that maybe killed my own father."

Ryan came up straight, his face going stiff and cold. He said: "Do you believe all those things you are saying?"

She half turned from him, tears all at once flooding her eyes. "What else can I believe? There's so much proof! You say Hugh wants to take over this ranch . . . this whole country, and that it was his man that killed my father. He says the same of you . . . that you plan to control the Vega by the power of your gun. Your first move was to get my father out of the way so you could take over the S-Bar. And now you will try to do the same with the Circle X, only your attempt to kill Hugh failed."

93

Jim Ryan waited patiently, hearing it out to the last word. It was the old pattern, the old divide-and-conquer theme, ageless as time itself. When he made his reply, his voice was low. "If that is what you believe, there's little use of me saying more. Only for your sake, be careful of Hugh. Don't trust him or any of those around him."

"Who, then, can I trust? Everything is so mixed up, so confused. I don't know who to trust any more."

"Only one man I'm sure of," Ryan said, "and that's Frank Sears. I'll send him to you tonight. Listen to him and do what he says."

In silence she nodded to him. Ryan touched her face with one last look and turned to go. She halted him with: "Where are you going now?"

A measure of the deep bitterness in the man rose to the surface. "Oh, just on. Would you like for me to tell you exactly so you could send Baldwin or Ross Meldrum after me?"

The stricken look that crossed her face shamed him in that moment. He said, more kindly: "Forget that. I'll send Frank over after dark. If there's one man in this country that is on the level and that you can trust, it's him."

He moved again to depart, steadying himself, as he pivoted, against the door.

"Will you be back?" she asked in a small voice.

He gave her a short, tight smile over his shoulder. "Not likely. Good bye, Ann."

# Chapter Thirteen

It was near the end of the afternoon when Ryan, having followed a devious route back along the creek, rounded a sharp bend in the green band of willows and other growth and came into view of the Box K. He stopped within the last extreme outthrusting of brush and let his gaze rove over the premises with deliberate thoroughness. It was still deserted, more so now for only Frank Sears's pony was to be seen. The horses of the two guards left by the posse were gone.

Evidently they had tired of fruitless waiting and had moved on, probably joining up with the others still somewhere along the bluffs. But Ryan, ever cautious, waited a time until he was convinced before he crossed the open ground and came in on the buildings from their blind side. He reached the main house, drifting quietly in from the yard's southern tip, and paused there at the corner, listening for voices, for any sounds. But the ranch was still as death. He wheeled the roan around and crossed by the front door, which was standing open, and pointed for the bunkhouse. Sears would most likely be there.

He came to a sudden stop. There, halfway out, lay the body of Frank Sears. A wide, ugly stain covered his back, starting just below the shoulders and spreading down to his hips. Ryan spun quickly toward the house and leaped off the roan. Gun in hand, he ducked into the kitchen doorway. From that shelter, he checked the rest of the ranch, the edging brush, the low hills to the west. But he could find nothing that appeared to be a hidden man. The thought came to him then that the killer, or killers, might possibly still be in the house.

He moved silently into the kitchen. A scatter of dirty dishes was on the table. The coffee pot was on the range, and Ryan moved to that, laying his hand on the stove lids. They were cold. There had been no fire in the range for hours.

He turned to the other rooms, treading softly down the hallway. Anger was a suppressed flame beginning to burn hotly within him. The rooms were all empty, and in each he found nothing but destruction: furniture smashed, walls kicked in, glass broken. The bedding had been ripped to shreds, the mattresses slashed, and the stuffings strewn about. In the parlor, where he kept his desk and that he used as a sort of office, the desk had been broken open and all his papers and records had been piled in the center of the room. A match had been set to them. The floor was burned almost through, and the smell of that still hung about the walls.

Satisfied, finally, that no one was hidden in the house, he made a check of the bunkhouse, the barn, and all the lesser sheds and structures, finding nothing. His face a grim mask, he returned to where Sears's body lay in the yard. A rumble of thunder sounded somewhere off to the east.

The old 'puncher lay face down, arms pinned beneath him. There were two bullet wounds in his back. Death had struck solidly as he apparently had been walking across the yard, going from the main building to the bunkhouse. Ryan, the roar of anger rising steadily within him, turned the body over gently.

Folded over one arm were the three fancy woolen shirts Ryan had given him. He remembered how Sears had always admired them. He had planned several times to put them in the hands of the man, but somehow he always forgot. He was glad he had made it plain, earlier in the day, that they were actually his and that he was to get them. Three fancy shirts—that was all the old rider had asked for his loyalty to the Box K before it passed on to someone else.

Ignoring his agonizing leg, Ryan slipped his arm under Sears's frail body and carried it into the bunkhouse. He laid it on the bed, straightened out the stiffening legs, and folded the arms over the chest. The shirts he placed nearby, and over it all he drew a blanket.

In the hot closeness he stood there, thinking deeply. His gaze reached out through the window to the sun-swept prairie, to the Santa Claras lifting their rugged bulks beyond. Men were still searching for him out there, men ready to shoot and kill him the moment they saw him. That was the chance any man took when things shaped up in that order. A man stood against his own enemies and took his chances with them, just as they did with him.

But to murder Frank Sears brutally! A harmless old man! To shoot him in the back as he walked, unarmed, across an open yard was another matter. They had had nothing against Sears, nothing other than that he was a friend of Ryan's. And that was little cause.

Anger was a brittle, moving force through Ryan, not a wild, furious blaze, but a deadly sort of cold determination. It pulled down the corners of his lips and made livid the area around his mouth. His eyes narrowed to a straight, dark line. Turning to look again at Sears, the thought moved him: *There's no leaving this thing now. There's no way out of it. A man can't turn his back on a mad dog or walk around a poisonous snake and sleep easy. Whether I want it or not, I'm in this thing because, in some way or another, it affects me. No matter where a man turns, I guess, there's a Hugh Baldwin knocking down a Frank Sears.*

He left the bunkhouse, the growling thunder to the east

rolling across the hot, late afternoon sky again. He went to the kitchen and rustled himself a fair amount of food from the shelves in the storeroom, selecting the kind that would not require any amount of cooking. He tossed this into a flour sack and to it added coffee and a small lard bucket to brew it in. He moved swiftly but methodically, wasting no motions, knowing it was dangerous to remain here for long. At any time Baldwin or some of his men or Ross Meldrum and members of the posse might return, and he was not ready just yet to meet them.

Completing his stores, he started for the yard and then remembered the canteen. He filled this from a bucket of water, brought in by Sears probably earlier in the day, and once again started to leave. Outside, he glanced to his gun belt. It was less than half filled. He placed the sack of grub and the canteen on the ground and reëntered the house, this time going to the front room, hoping Baldwin's men had passed up the closet.

They had not entirely, as the clothing tossed to the floor proved. But the shelf was still up and they had not found the two boxes of cartridges stashed in one corner. He thrust the boxes into his pocket and went back into the ranch yard.

The roan had drifted to the water trough. Ryan crossed that distance with his load, limping heavily. He wished there was something he could do to ease the wound, but there seemed to be nothing more except to stay off of it. And that, of course, was out of the question now.

He crammed the sack of grub into one saddlebag, the canteen in the other, making sure no sounds of metal would arise when the roan moved. He filled his empty cartridge belt to capacity from the box of shells, folding those left over into a handkerchief and tucking them into a shirt pocket. The remaining box he also put in a saddlebag.

Ready at last, he swung to the saddle, settling his injured leg slowly into the stirrup. He glanced to the west—at least two hours remained before sundown. Time enough to get back within the shelter along Willow Creek before it became fully dark. There he would eat a little, and after that he would travel, heading north for Circle X and Hugh Baldwin.

# Chapter Fourteen

Ryan delayed until night had fully settled before starting upstream. Deep in the tangle of willows and brier, he ate from the food he had brought, denying himself, however, the strength and comfort of coffee. A fire's glare or its plume of smoke, no matter how small, might be seen and lead searchers to his camp. Physically he was feeling fairly strong again. The man's immense vitality, that hard, stringy core of strength that came from a life of rugged, outdoor living under all conditions, was making its own repairs and recoveries. He required little help from outside measures for healing.

When he swung up on the roan, he had almost forgotten the wound in his leg, but the sharp pain that shot through him when he came too solidly against the leather was a pointed reminder that it was still tender and weak. Nevertheless, it had greatly improved over the previous night. There was still some stiffness, and the soreness was to be expected. By another sunset, he realized, the leg would be in good condition if he could keep it from becoming overtaxed and the wound broken open again.

Ryan, however, was wasting little thought upon it. In his mind there now existed a single, solitary purpose—get Hugh Baldwin, bring him in to face up to his actions. He was the match that had started the flames of range fire; he was the power behind the killing of Tom Strickland and now Frank Sears. And there would be many more if he was left to go on. Pull down Baldwin now! That was the only answer. To break up his empire before it became an entrenched, towering reality blighting the Vega—that was the need of the hour.

It was because Hugh Baldwin was already so strong, so powerful a figure, that made the doing difficult. The threat of him and his ruthless Circle X riders had laid a firm grasp upon the minds of almost all who lived in the shadow of the ridge. Tom Strickland had bucked against that yoke, and now he was dead. This they all already knew, and that full knowledge would make them careful, turn them fearful.

Ryan concluded then that it likely would have been he who next would have been slated to fall. The way things happened served only to simplify and bring him into the picture sooner. Had he not been at Strickland's that day and thus walked conveniently into Baldwin's plans and a charge of murder, Baldwin would have gotten around to him later. In a way it was all to the good. Now he was forewarned, and the advantage of surprise was lost to Hugh Baldwin. Actually, it now lay with Ryan. And Jim Ryan, wise to the ways of men like Baldwin, knew well how to use such a weapon.

He met no riders on his steady journey up the creek. When he came to the Strickland bridge, he paused as he had done earlier in the day, an impulse to see Ann pulling at him. For a time he studied the squares of yellow light scattered among the buildings, and then, reaching a decision, he put the roan to a soft trot toward the windbreak. Reaching the cover of the tamarisks, he advanced more slowly until he was close to the main house.

The shade was drawn upon the window closest to him. Ignoring the possible danger, he drifted across the front of the house and down the side to where the kitchen lay. That window was still open, and he pulled up outside it, just beyond its gush of light. Ann was there at the table, reading a thick, black-bound book.

Lamplight lay across her serene face. Her lips were set in

soft, curving lines, and, when she moved slightly, the blackness of her hair reflected the light and glinted brightly. Every man has his own conception of personal paradise in which all ideals have come to pass and all desires are fulfilled. Ryan knew then, in that moment, Ann Strickland constituted a major factor in his idea of paradise. And he had the realization in that same moment that such was not now likely ever to be his. He was a man alone, one of the friendless. The last of those few he might call friend lay dead in his own bunkhouse. He was completely and utterly alone, with all the country turned against him, or else fearing to help. And he was undertaking a mission from which he might never return. But even if it came to that, there would be some satisfaction in the knowledge that he had eliminated Hugh Baldwin from the land.

A door slammed, somewhere off to the left. He let his glance rest upon Ann for another run of seconds and then wheeled the blue toward the tamarisks.

A voice broke the stillness: "Who's that? Who's out there?"

Ryan touched the roan with spurs, and the blue leaped away.

"What's goin' on out there?" George Cobb's voice took up the challenge.

Ryan reached the windbreak and dropped quickly into its tangled depths. The blue had to move more slowly now but so would any pursuers, if there were to be any. He came out on the opposite side and waited there, listening into the night. He heard the distant drumbeats of thunder, farther away than it had been earlier, and also another slam of a door. That was all. Whoever might have seen him had not been sure, and the other men in the S-Bar bunkhouse likely were having their joke with him at that moment.

★ ★ ★ ★ ★

Circle X lay deep in the bottom of a grassy bowl. A few trees ringed the place, and along the back, where a spring bubbled from the rocks, there was a stand of bayberry and thick-growing willows. Ryan directed the roan into that. He had been to Circle X only once before, attending a meeting of cattle growers when there was a shipping problem to be ironed out. He sat there now in the full darkness, trying to remember all he knew about the spread.

It was laid out much like his own Box K, which was a fairly common plan or arrangement in that part of the West. The main house, a long, rambling structure, was on the right, facing east. The bunkhouse stood across a hard-packed yard, and behind it lay a scatter of small buildings, corrals, pens, and sheds. Finishing it all off was the barn. Baldwin would be in the main house at this hour. Supper would be over, and the crew either in their bunks or gathered there, shooting the breeze about the events of the day.

The question was: would Baldwin be alone, or would some of the men be with him?

Ryan drifted the roan out of the willows and reached the extreme rear of the main house. Pausing there to listen, he heard nothing and pressed on once more until he had reached the front. Here he dismounted and left the blue standing just out of sight in deep shadows, reins looped over a stunted juniper.

He took three steps forward and then froze against the wall of the house, hearing the sudden, rapid approach of riders. They rushed into the yard, four of them cutting away toward the bunkhouse, while two pulled up at the rail in front, not fifteen feet from where Ryan stood. They stepped down, and in the splash of light coming from the open door he recognized Reno Davis and the huge bulk of Turk Paulson. A blunt, red welt lay across Paulson's face, running from temple to cheek-bone, showing where Ryan's gun had laid its mark.

"Hugh!" Davis sang out his greeting and came up on the narrow porch. He did not pull open the door and enter, but waited for Baldwin's invitation. Turk Paulson thumped up behind him, rubbing at his neck in a reflective sort of fashion.

"Hey, Hugh!"

"All right, all right," Baldwin's voice came from the center of the house. "Come in and set. I'll be with you in a minute."

Davis and Paulson entered, the big man letting the screen door bang loudly behind him. Ryan heard Davis swear softly at that and then caught Paulson's rumbling reply. He moved around to where he could hear better. The window shade was pulled down tight, and he could see nothing. But he was content with his position—to move farther out where he might see better would be too risky.

Baldwin came into the room. Ryan heard the chair creak under his weight and his deep-throated voice say: "Well? You get him?"

"Not yet," Reno Davis answered. "Turk, here, saw him."

"Saw him?" Baldwin echoed. "How come you didn't nail him?"

"Never had no chance," Paulson grumbled. "He tried to run me down with that big horse of his, and then beat my head in with a gun butt."

"And what the hell were you doing all that time? Where was your horse? What were you doing to him?"

The dull wits of Turk Paulson could not match the speed of the questions. "I reckon I fell off, Mister Baldwin," he stammered out slowly. "I was tryin'. . . ."

"Fell off!" Hugh Baldwin's words exploded from his lips. "The only man to see Ryan in two days and he falls off his damn' horse! What kind of men you got working for me, Reno?"

"Somebody else will find him," Davis said soothingly. "He's bound to show up soon. He can't hole up much longer with a bullet in his hide."

"Who's watching his place?"

"Couple of them new hands . . . Pete Santee and Al Thompson. They drilled old Sears."

"Sears? Why?"

"Don't know for sure. Turk and me found him layin' out there in the yard. Pete and Al was arguin' about leavin'."

"Running out, eh? What's got into them?"

"Reckon old Sears was the first man they'd ever cut down. Guess their feet was gettin' a little cold."

"You change their minds?"

Davis laughed. "We sure did! They changed their minds all right, after me and Turk got done talkin' to them."

"What about Sears?"

"Left him layin' there."

"Good . . . good thinking, Reno," Baldwin said. "That'll put the fear of God in some of these weak-kneed ones and maybe change the minds of any others who may have ideas. How many of the boys still on the job?"

"Five, and the marshal's still got some of his posse workin'. They're beginnin' to peter out, though. We better catch this Ryan by tomorrow night, or I figure we'll be doin' this all alone."

"We'll have him by then," Baldwin stated, assuming some of Davis's earlier confidence. "One more night with a bullet hole in his guts will make a lot of difference. I figure he'll show up tomorrow crying for help."

"Maybe you're right," Davis said, now seemingly unsure of Ryan's inevitable capture. "But the workin' over he give

Turk here don't look to me like a man ready to cash in."

"Strength of a desperate man," Baldwin dismissed it. "Probably put everything he had left into it. Now, first thing in the morning you take Turk and a couple of the boys and go back to where Turk saw him . . . to where Turk fell off his horse," he added with heavy sarcasm.

Ryan heard the big man grumble and shift about on his feet.

Baldwin continued: "Work the brush over close. My guess is you'll find him crawled in under a bush, dead."

"Could be," Reno Davis murmured.

Ryan heard the scrape of chairs upon the floor as the men got up. The ponderous bulk of Turk Paulson blocked the doorway briefly and then moved out onto the porch. Davis followed.

"I'll ride down first thing I can and see what you've found," Baldwin called after them. "Now, get down there early."

"Sure . . . early, Hugh," Davis replied, and crossed the porch. Paulson let the door bang shut again, and Davis expressed his feelings once more in a single, withering word. Together they thumped across the hard pack. Ryan waited until they had entered the bunkhouse, then, drawing his gun, he covered the porch's width in a half dozen long, stealthy strides.

Baldwin sat deep in a cushioned chair, relaxed, studying the backs of his broad hands. Ryan stepped inside the room like a swift shadow. Baldwin looked up, surprise breaking through his eyes but blank in his expression.

Ryan said: "Get up, Hugh, we're riding to town."

# Chapter Fifteen

For a short, breathless space of time Hugh Baldwin made no sound. Somewhere in the depths of the house, a clock ticked loudly. Outside, at the hitching rail, one of the horses blew and stamped wearily. Gradually the look of incredulity faded from Baldwin's face, and his gaze firmed up and locked with that of Jim Ryan's.

"That's a mighty big order," he said.

"Not with you helping," Ryan answered coolly.

Baldwin smiled, the old cocksure confidence once again threading through his voice. "Just how far do you think you'll get . . . walking across that yard with a gun in my back?"

"Guess again," Ryan said softly. "We're not crossing any yard. You're going to get up and go quiet out the door and mount up one of those horses standing there at the rail."

"And then?"

"My horse is around at the side. We'll get him and go into town."

"What for? I don't understand what you want me in town for."

Ryan said harshly: "The hell you don't, Hugh! Cut out the stalling. It's late. And you know as well as I do that nobody's going to be coming over here before daylight."

Baldwin shook his head. "Still don't know what you want me in town for."

"Several things. Mainly, I'm going to fit you into place so everybody can see who and what you really are in this country. Then you're going to explain why you had Tom

Strickland and Frank Sears killed."

Baldwin said—"Frank Sears?"—in a wondering way.

Ryan shrugged impatiently. "Don't give me that, Hugh. Reno and Turk just told you about it. I heard everything they had to say." Ryan paused, the glitter in his eyes hardened, and the lines around his mouth became deep, rigid cuts. "Sears was a friend of mine," he said. "One of the few honest men I've ever known. If I didn't have any other reason in the world to want to see you swing, I'd drop everything for that one."

Baldwin sighed. His eyes gave Ryan a close, hard scrutiny. "I didn't know about Sears until it was all over," he said. Then: "Ryan, I wish you'd think about this thing. I'd give a pretty penny to have a man like you working for me. I need a man of your cut . . . somebody that's got some sense and can think for himself."

"For what you're trying to do, you need a lot of men, a lot of things," Ryan said dryly.

"What makes you so sure Sears is dead? Reno didn't say that. He said he'd been shot."

"I was there," Ryan answered. "I found him in the yard, two bullets in the back. I carried him into the bunkhouse. He's dead, Hugh."

"And you did all this and my boys didn't see you?"

"Your boys had run. Left you flat."

A change of expression moved fleetingly across the cattleman's face, first of surprise, and then one of slight worry. It was as if he were seeing the first crack in a wall he had thought impregnable. "Gone?"

"Gone," Ryan echoed. "They'd had all they wanted of this deal. Maybe they saw what was sure to come, and they didn't want to be on hand when it got here."

"Coming? Nothing's coming," Baldwin declared flatly.

"They were just yellow. Things got a little rough, and they didn't have the guts for it. Good men are hard to come by nowadays."

Ryan shook his head. "Maybe, the kind you want. But good men are plentiful. And they'll have a few things to say when they stand you up before them. Get up, Hugh. We're going out of here now."

Baldwin rose to his feet. Small beads of sweat on his brow betrayed the calmness on his face, and his hands trembled slightly. He nodded to the gun held ready by Ryan.

"You're not horsing me any, Ryan. If I make a break, you wouldn't dare pull that trigger. One shot and you'd have a dozen men down on your head."

"Something you wouldn't live to see, Hugh," Ryan said with a tight smile. "You'd be a dead man long before that first half minute was up. Let's go." Ryan stepped aside and motioned to Baldwin.

The cattleman moved toward the door.

"Walk slow. Go out to the rail and take one of those horses. Don't make any unnecessary noise doing it. I'll be three feet behind you, my gun pointed at your backbone. Make a quick move in the wrong direction or try and sing out and you'll never know what hit you."

Baldwin was sweating freely, and some of his confidence had fled. "You'll never get away with this," he said, but it was more to assure himself than deter Ryan.

"We'll see," Ryan murmured softly. "Move."

Baldwin crossed before Ryan, dragging his steps. He pushed back the screen door and walked onto the porch. He was in his stocking feet, and he made no sound other than his deep, labored breathing. Ryan caught the door and closed it gently.

"Hold it, Hugh," he said in a quick, low voice.

For a minute he stood there, a rigid, square, black shape, listening into the darkness. The yard was stone quiet, almost too quiet, it seemed to him.

He said: "Take the reins of that first horse. Don't mount up. Lead him around to the side of the house. I can watch you better while you're walking."

"Not my horse," Baldwin said in a mild, protesting way as he moved to comply.

In the quiet, Ryan smiled grimly at the workings of the man's mind. "Makes no difference now," he said. "Whoever owns him will get him back."

"Reno's horse," Baldwin grumbled. He pulled the leathers free of the rail and turned to Ryan. "Now what?"

"You know what I said . . . lead him around to the side. And do it slow. I'm right behind you."

Ryan pulled back to let Baldwin pass by. The night was crackling with tension, and the stillness was solid enough to feel. Ryan kept his gun close to the cattleman. He was not sure of him, not certain if he would follow orders or would make a break for it. He did not want the man dead, and he was hoping Baldwin would come along without trouble. But he was prepared to shoot if necessary.

Baldwin moved slowly while leading the pony. He cast a sidelong glance at Ryan, and in the faint light Ryan could see the heavy shine of sweat upon his forehead and cheeks and across his upper lip. "Walk slow, Hugh," he warned in a dead-level voice.

Whatever qualities Hugh Baldwin lacked, one of them was not courage. In the complete stillness of the night, he made his desperate move. Ryan saw him lunge at the horse, a shadowy outline in the gloom. He saw the horse's head go down as Baldwin wrenched at the reins. The animal, startled, pivoted wildly, its hindquarters swinging at Ryan. Ryan stepped back hurriedly, forgetting his weak leg. He half fell.

"Reno!" Baldwin yelled.

The summons rocked through the yard and echoed against the buildings. The back door flung open, and Davis and three or four other men pounded into the open.

"Hugh? That you yellin'? What's up?" Davis's voice lifted into the night.

Ryan, back on his feet like a cat, moved in against Baldwin. He jammed the barrel of his gun into the man's ribs.

"Answer him, quick. Tell him everything's all right. Quick, damn you."

Davis came trotting across the yard. He stopped in front of the house, uncertain. Ryan saw him throw a glance at the rail and note the missing horse. But he seemed a little in doubt. "What's wrong, Hugh?"

"Nothing, nothing," Baldwin replied in a rasping voice. "Everything's all right, Reno."

"Who's out there with you?"

Ryan dug the gun barrel deeper. Baldwin winced. "A friend, Reno. That's all. Just a friend."

"Little late for a social call," Davis murmured into the night. The others had turned and were drifting back to the bunkhouse. Davis hung on. "Anything you want, Hugh?"

Ryan did not miss the hard note of suspicion coloring the 'puncher's tone. He was not convinced, not fooled one minute. But Baldwin's answers had him pinned down. He was at a loss as to what he should do.

Baldwin said: "Never mind, Reno. Go on back to bed."

Davis turned about slowly to follow the others. Ryan watched him closely as he crossed the dimly lit hard pack and enter the bunkhouse. He saw the door close, and almost in the same instant the light went out. Something wasn't right. He could feel it even though he could not put his finger exactly on it. To Baldwin he said: "Now, Hugh, we'll move on. That was your last false move. This is a one-time deal, and the next time you try anything, I won't bother to wait."

Baldwin made no reply. He gathered up the reins of the horse and moved around the corner of the house. Ryan watched him narrowly, the flags of danger still waving in his mind. He again had that strong feeling that something was not exactly right, but he was still unable to pin it down. For one thing, he had no way of knowing how many men had come from the bunkhouse in response to Baldwin's summons, and he did not know if they had all returned. It was possible they could have split, and some circled the house and were now waiting ahead in the deep blackness where the roan stood.

Ryan shrugged. Little matter now. He was this far, and there could be no turning back those last few minutes. If they did jump him, Baldwin was due to get his first bullet. He would do the Vega that favor before they cut him down.

Ahead, Baldwin stumbled in the darkness, cursing softly. Ryan said: "Slow, Hugh. Take it slow. No hurry now."

It seemed far longer to the point where he had left the roan. Baldwin stopped there, and Ryan slipped past him, keeping his gun leveled at the Circle X owner's breast. "When I get in the saddle, you mount up," he said. "And do it slow and easy-like."

Reno Davis's voice cracked suddenly through the darkness. "Nobody's mountin' up! 'Specially you, Ryan!"

Ryan squeezed the trigger of his gun. The report shattered the night, and the orange flare-up was a brief, vivid, and blinding flash. But Baldwin had lunged away into the brush, keeping the horse between himself and Ryan. The bullet went wild. Davis fired in the next breath, and Ryan felt the heat of the lead scorch his cheek. He ducked away, wheeling toward that man.

Davis's bantering voice said: "Come on, Ryan! Come on in close! You're an easy target! Where'd you like to have it? In the head? In the belly?"

Baldwin's strong voice broke in from the shadows on the right. "Hold it up, Reno. I want that jasper alive. Where the hell's that light?"

Several Circle X men closed in, one bearing a lantern. He had been pretty well surrounded, Ryan noted. Baldwin came into the group.

"You were a long time getting here," he said sourly to Davis.

"When there's shootin' to be done, I like to pick my own time and place," Davis replied coolly.

Baldwin swung to Ryan. He reached over and wrenched the gun from his hand. "Out front, friend. And don't *you* make any false moves. There's a dozen guns looking at you. You wouldn't have the luck I had."

Ryan headed for the yard, hearing the others fall in behind him. Near the center of the hard pack, Baldwin said—"Hold it!"—and he stopped. "Turn around!"

Ryan pivoted slowly on his good leg. The roan was being led over to the corral and tied up. Nine men, he ticked them off methodically, stood in a half circle with Baldwin, enclosing him. Eleven in all, counting the rider looking after the blue. This must be the entire crew. The gunshots would have brought everybody out.

Baldwin said: "Well, Ryan, like I tried to tell you, you cut yourself a big piece of pie. Too big to swallow. I told you that you'd never get away with it."

Ryan shrugged. "Not over yet, Hugh."

"For you, yes. I've got all I need now. I'll keep you under cover for a couple more days to give me time to finish up a few things. That way Meldrum and his posse will keep out from under foot. When I'm ready, I'll take you in. You just dealt yourself a hand in a game way too big for you."

Ryan said: "No, you're wrong there. It's the other way around. You dealt me in when you tried to frame me for Strickland's murder."

Baldwin chuckled. "Can't see that it makes much difference since we're playing my game." He turned to Reno Davis. "Put him in that old shed next to the bunkhouse. And keep a watch over him. He's a smart one."

Davis said: "Turk, here's your playmate. You hear what Mister Baldwin said?"

Paulson shuffled out into the fan of light where Ryan waited. His mouth was split into a wicked, happy grin. His big hands swung like huge hams at his sides. "I heard."

"I want him alive," Baldwin said, eyeing the big man sharply. "Watch yourself now, Turk."

"Yes, sir, I heard," Paulson said, and swung his balled fist like a club.

Ryan tried to duck, but the blow caught him fully on the ear. Lights flashed through the darkness, and the sound of laughter rushed loudly in and then faded swiftly away into a void. That was all he remembered.

# Chapter Sixteen

Sometime near midnight, Ryan came back to his senses. He remained quiet, feeling the solid throb of his head and the steady, dull ache in his leg. The dry crustiness there told him the wound had burst open, bled, and now was again closed.

Hearing no sound but the rasping of his own breath, he sat up. The rush of pain behind his eyes almost turned him sick, and he sat there motionless, holding his face between his hands while the nausea passed. After a few minutes he felt somewhat better. He glanced about the small room. It was only dimly lit, there being no other light save feeble starshine. He was alone, and the room was barren except for the hard cot upon which he sat.

Back toward the ridge a gunshot sounded, distant and empty. And somewhere on Circle X premises a dog began to bark. Ryan settled down on the cot, too tired to listen, too tired to look farther, and too sick to think much about the things that had happened. His throat was dry, and he wished he had a drink of water, but there was none to be had in the shed, and he knew it would be useless to call out.

When he again opened his eyes, he felt much better. The blinding headache, memento of Turk Paulson's punishing roundhouse blow, had dwindled to minor proportions, and there was only a thin string of pain running through his leg to remind him of that injury. Warm sunlight streamed through the streaky glass of the single window, flooding the cell-like quarters, and he was already aware that the stuffy closeness was beginning to grow. He got unsteadily to his feet and crossed to the window. It was down, shut tight, and he slammed the lower half open.

Instantly Turk Paulson was there. He came from the front where, apparently, he had been keeping guard at the door. His pig eyes sparked their suspicion, and he had a gun in his big fist.

Ryan grinned at him—"Hot in here."—and moved back to the cot.

Paulson grumbled something inaudible and returned to his post. Ryan gave him five minutes to settle down and moved softly back to the window. He laid a sharp glance over the yard, the corral, and the main house. Men were moving about, doing their early chores. In front of the barn, fresh horses were being saddled for the day's use. The cook came out of a side door near the end of the building and rapped on a triangular gong with a claw hammer and returned quickly inside.

Riders began to drift toward the kitchen. Ryan counted them off. Seven. Paulson at the door of the shed made eight. Baldwin, inside, would raise it to nine. Two missing from last night's count. They showed up at that moment, coming from the depths of the barn where they had been working.

Ryan returned to the cot but checked himself when he heard the pound of hoofs. Four men rode into the yard. They pulled up before the corral, slapped their horses through the gate, and disappeared immediately into the house. The rest of the crew, Ryan guessed. But he could not be sure. Circle X was a large spread and fourteen hands could be right, or it could be considerably short. Men of Baldwin's stripe like plenty of help. It could be that this was only the floating crew. There might be several more men out working the range.

For the first time Ryan thought back over the night's events. He questioned himself as to his wisdom in attempting to take Baldwin in. In the cold, brutal light of failure it seemed to him now there must have been some other, better way to accomplish what he had tried. But, even at this point, he could not think of what it would be. He was a man of direct, simple action, prone to move on straightforward lines when necessity dictated. And, as a result, he seldom indulged in regrets for something gone awry. The gain, to his way of thinking, far outweighed the risk in times such as this, and that was the important thing to be considered.

He heard the screen door bang at the kitchen and then the sound of boot heels rapping across the hard pack. Glancing out, he saw Reno Davis approaching, and he moved back to the cot and sat down.

The door kicked back, and Davis said: "Grub. In the kitchen."

He ducked his head toward the main house and stepped back, watching Ryan with a surly intentness. Outside, Paulson waited in dumb silence. Ryan walked into the open, moving swiftly but with some difficulty.

"Come on, come on," Davis said testily. "Ain't got the whole day. You eat, too, Turk."

Ryan started across the yard, followed closely by Davis and Paulson. Men were coming out of the kitchen, pausing along the step to roll their cigarettes or pick their teeth and watch. Ryan halted near the door and placed his gaze on one of the riders.

"Appreciate your feeding and watering my horse," he said. "He's been standing there at that fence all night."

The man eyed Ryan carefully. With a half smile, he said: "Why? You figurin' on goin' somewheres?"

Several of the others laughed, and Ryan moved on. But when he glanced back, he saw the man heading for the roan to carry out his request.

There was no one in the kitchen, when they entered. Ryan sat down at a clean plate, and Paulson took a chair almost directly opposite. Reno Davis made a stand near the door, never removing his sulky gaze from Ryan's form. The cook entered bringing two platters heaped with eggs and fried meat. He left these to return shortly with a pan of hot biscuits and a pot of steaming hot coffee.

Ryan drank a cup of the scalding brew almost without pausing. It seared his throat and warmed his belly, and immediately, it seemed, he felt much better. He refilled the cup. The loosening of the tightness in his muscles was a most welcome sensation. He glanced at Paulson who wolfed his food in great gulps.

Davis said: "Better eat, friend. You may be a long time gettin' the next meal."

Ryan turned to the eggs and meat. He was hungry, and he ate steadily, washing the food down with some more of the strong, black coffee. When he was finished, he leaned back from the table. Paulson continued to eat.

Ryan looked at Davis. "Any chance for a smoke?"

Davis tossed him the makings. Ryan rolled a deft cigarette and started to get up. Davis stopped him. "Never mind that. Just throw it."

Ryan shrugged, threw the makings to Davis, and settled back. Outside the crew was bringing up the horses. Baldwin was there. Ryan heard his voice overriding all other sounds.

"Tip, you take six of the boys and get back to Meldrum and the posse. Keep them looking for Ryan. Say you heard he was farther back on the ridge. I want the marshal and his bunch out of the way for a couple more days."

Ryan heard the men mount up and rush out of the yard. The door opened and Baldwin thrust his head inside. "You about through in here, Reno?"

"Waitin' on Turk," Davis grumbled. "Man eats like a horse."

"Well, hurry it up. Get Ryan back in that shed. Time we were moving."

"You heard him," Davis said, throwing a glance at Ryan and motioning him to the door. To Paulson he said: "Come on, Turk. You'll have another chance at it tonight."

Ryan stepped into the yard. Baldwin awaited him with sly humor in his eyes. The others of the crew stood by in expectant silence.

"Pretty tame this morning," Baldwin said. "Not the ringtailed cat you were last night."

Ryan pulled up in front of the cattleman and faced him. He reached the cigarette from his lips and flicked it straight at Baldwin. Baldwin swore and stepped quickly back, brushing ashes and tobacco from his shirt while the color in his neck flushed red.

Davis crowded in at once, dragging at his gun, but Baldwin stopped him. "Never mind, Reno. Not time for that now." He turned to Ryan. "Too bad you can't see it my way. I like a man with guts. We'd make a good team."

Ryan shrugged. "Wrong team, Hugh. Your kind never runs far enough. And never fast enough to get away."

Baldwin considered that for a moment. He smiled. "We'll see," he said. "Tuck him away, Reno."

Ryan started for his cell. He heard Davis say: "You want Turk to stay with him again?"

And Baldwin's reply: "No, let Turk get some sleep. Put Halverson there."

That man, a squat, powerful rider built much along the same lines as Reno Davis, came off his horse and followed along to the shed. Ryan entered and heard the door snap shut behind.

Davis's voice said: "If he makes a break for it, cut him down. Hugh says keep him alive, but I don't hold with that. He's too damn' cute to take a chance with, and, far as I'm concerned, you can do anything you want. Just don't let him get out of here alive."

Halverson grunted some sort of reply, and Davis thumped away. In a moment he was back, coming to the window. "Ryan, thought maybe you'd like to know where we're headed . . . to your place. When we get back, you'll be ownin' a nice pile of ashes."

Davis wheeled away, and Ryan, standing at the window, watched him mount up and wait with the others for Baldwin. After a few minutes the cattleman came out, dressed in some sort of fine, gray material and wearing a broad white hat. His boots glistened blackly in the sunlight as he stepped to the saddle. They rode out in a body, striking south.

Ryan settled down on the cot, and the morning dragged on, hour trailing hour. The shed grew hotter with its trapped heat, and Ryan finally went to the door and swung it open. Halverson was alert at once, his gun pointing straight at Ryan's breastbone.

Ryan said calmly: "Plenty hot in here. Like to leave this open for a spell."

Halverson wagged his head. "Close it. And don't make no more sudden moves like that if you want to keep livin'."

Ryan kicked the door shut and returned to the window. At least the roan was getting fed and watered and was in out of the sun. He tried to see where they had taken him, but he was not in sight. Likely he was in the barn. Ryan tried then to gauge his chances for escape. Halverson, of course, was the big obstacle, waiting there outside the door.

Turk Paulson would be in the bunkhouse asleep. He wished Baldwin had left the big man on guard, but Baldwin was too smart for that. He had realized Ryan probably would try and trick the slow-witted giant, and he was taking no chances on it working. The cook was somewhere in the main house. A thought came to him then, and he remembered the four men who had come in later. Where were they? He swiveled his glance to the corral. Their horses were still there, saddled and waiting. Apparently, like Turk Paulson, they were catching up on a little sleep.

If only he could figure out a way to get by Halverson and not kick up a row that would awaken the sleeping men. It would be easy, after that. But how to get by Halverson? That was the big problem.

He was still threshing it around in his mind, casting in all directions for some answer, when the crew returned. It must have been around two o'clock. Looking through the open window, he saw Hugh Baldwin was not with them, and he had his own quick guess as to where that man had gone, dressed as he was. Reno Davis rode straight to the shed and, leaning from the saddle, called to Ryan.

"Like I promised, you own a mighty nice pile of ashes, cowboy. Made a right pretty fire."

"My stock?" Ryan asked.

"We're lookin' after them. We're letting them run with some good Circle X stuff."

Ryan waited a moment. Then: "Frank Sears's body was in the bunkhouse. You bury him before you burned the place?"

Davis grinned. "He went up in smoke just like all the rest of it. What's the difference? One way's as good as another. He didn't know nothin' about it, anyway."

Ryan pulled back from the window, disgusted and a little sick at what he had heard. Any man deserved a decent burial, and he particularly would have liked for Sears to have had one. The deep, glowing anger for Hugh Baldwin increased its intensity. He had realized once more that he was too exposed; he had realized...

He heard Halverson near the corner of the building say: "Didn't see the boss come back. What happened to him?"

"Stopped off at that Strickland gal's place," Davis answered, turning away. "Reckon we'll by payin' her a call tonight if she don't see things his way."

Ryan settled down on the cot, his mind now racing desperately with his problem. There had to be a way out, a means for getting by Halverson. He had to think of something, and think of it soon.

# Chapter Seventeen

Baldwin rode in sometime later. He pulled up in front of the main house, tied his horse there, and, pausing, shouted—"Reno!"—then went inside.

Davis went trotting across from the bunkhouse and entered through the kitchen. Darkness was falling early. Masses of heavy, full-bellied clouds again piled up over the peaks and ridges of the Santa Claras and hung low above the prairie. The heat was holding, a stuffy sort of heat with the threat of rain riding with it. Examining the sky, Ryan saw the first streak of lightning stab through the overcast. The slow rumble of thunder was a distant, hushed sound.

*A few hours earlier and it might have saved my place,* Ryan thought, watching the storm gather. Davis came from the kitchen, the slam of the door overly loud in the pre-storm calmness. He headed directly for the bunkhouse, and, when he came out again, the others were close on his heels. Some, heeding the warnings grumbling overhead, were carrying their yellow slickers. Others were not bothering.

Davis detoured toward the shed. Ryan heard him say to Halverson: "We're movin' in on Strickland's."

"The gal wouldn't listen, eh?"

"I wouldn't know. Reckon not. Anyway, she must have said a few things that stuck in his craw. He's in no humor to talk about it."

"I got to stay here and watch this jasper?" Halverson asked after that.

"Somebody's got to. Might as well be you."

"Why can't Turk do it? He likes it."

"Uhn-uh," Davis said at once. "Baldwin's scared to leave him alone here. That bird would have him talked into ridin' into town before we got out of sight. Turk ain't got all he's supposed to upstairs."

"But it's goin' to rain!" Halverson protested. "What'll I do about that? I can't set out here in the wet."

"Then get inside with him. Only . . . watch him. Don't give him no chance to jump you."

"Don't worry about that. He won't get even half a chance," Halverson said.

Davis said: "Don't pay to be too sure about anything when you're foolin' with that one."

"What can he do? He's crippled up, and there ain't nothin' in there he could jump a man with. What you so worried about?"

"Just don't give him any chances," Davis said, and turned away.

Ryan smiled tightly and glanced through the window at the blackening sky. Rain had helped him once—that night when he had escaped into the hills. Maybe it would be that way again. Maybe his luck would run good once more. He pivoted slowly, making another careful search of the room, of the walls, of everything in it. He needed something with which to fight. A weapon of some sort, anything, anything at all that might be used. But the room was barren as a slab of granite.

He heard then the clatter of horses in the yard. This was followed by a low run of voices and grunts as the men swung up to the saddle. From the window, he watched Hugh Baldwin come out, dressed now in rough working clothes, and take his horse from Davis. He could not see too well in the rapidly dwindling light, but he counted the riders. He took a deep breath. They were all there, ready to leave, except for Halverson.

The first drops of rain began to pelt down, rapping loudly on the shed's thin roof. Two of the crew made a hurried break for the bunkhouse, deciding they would need their slickers, after all. Davis dismounted and hurried to fetch Baldwin's. Halverson grumbled his discomfort from beyond the door.

Ryan, watching the crew assemble, suddenly had his answer. He glanced down to the heavy gun belt still around his waist. They had taken his gun from him the night before in the yard, but they had not bothered to strip him of his cartridge belt. Unbuckling it, he slipped the holster off and tucked it under the cot. Doubling the belt, to form a sort of club, he sat down on the cot and made a few tentative slaps at his open palm. The folded leather made an efficient weapon.

The clatter of raindrops increased, and water began to slide down the walls where time and the sun's drying rays had warped loose the roof joists. A screech of metal against metal came from Halverson, and he knew the man was lighting a lantern against the closing darkness.

Reno Davis's voice lifted above the tumult, and Ryan heard the Circle X crew move out, turning south out of the yard. He remained seated, figuring Halverson would soon come. And he was now ready. He had a weapon with which to fight. It would be a gamble, long odds, but considering what lay ahead for him, when Hugh Baldwin was through, it was worth it. He hoped Halverson would not wait too long; he didn't want Baldwin and his riders to get too good a start on him.

"Hey . . . you in there . . . Ryan?"

Halverson's voice came through the door. Ryan waited a time before answering. Then: "Yeah? What do you want?"

"Where you at?"

"On the cot, trying to catch some sleep. Sure could use a blanket."

"Stay there," Halverson directed. "I'm comin' in out of this rain. I've got a gun in my hand. Don't make any false moves!"

"Come ahead," Ryan answered, and set himself for sudden, desperate action.

Halverson kicked back the door and entered. He carried the lantern in his left hand, leveled gun in the other. Water ran down his face and dropped on his chest and plastered his shirt against his barrel-like body. A small rivulet trickled off his hat and fell to the floor. He booted the door shut.

"You look pretty wet," Ryan remarked.

Halverson said sourly—"Stay right where you are."—and set the lantern in the corner.

"Sure," Ryan murmured agreeably and lunged to his feet. He struck with the folded gun belt, all in one, single motion, aiming at Halverson's head.

Pain roared through Ryan as he came down on his injured leg. It gave under his sudden weight, and, in so doing, it saved his life. Halverson's gun shattered the quiet, deafening them both within the confines of the small room. The bullet whistled by Ryan as he went down, and *thunked* dully into the floor. The belt missed Halverson's head, but it caught him across the neck and arms and knocked the gun away. It went skating across the floor, with Halverson clawing frantically after it.

Ryan caught the man by one foot and brought him hurtling down. Halverson struck out at him as he fell, but Ryan rolled away, taking the blow on his shoulder. He lashed out with both fists at the same time, using them like a club. Halverson grunted as Ryan kneed him in the belly. He lashed out for Ryan's face, searching for his eyes with probing fingers, but Ryan twisted around, getting free. Halverson's fingers caught his hair and began to pull back his head. In that same moment, he felt the Circle X rider's throat and clamped down. They pulled together and began to roll, locked to each other like that, around the floor.

They crashed full tilt against the cot, Ryan wincing as his bad leg took the brunt of the impact. He heaved, and they broke apart, Halverson coming out on top, breathing hard. Ryan felt the man digging again at his throat. He struggled to throw off the heavy, solid weight pressing him down, but he was lying at an angle and could not get the necessary leverage. He flailed out with both hands, trying to strike Halverson's face, but his efforts fell short.

The man's powerful fingers were closing him off, shutting out the drumming of the rain, the quick rasping of his own strained breathing. He threw his arms wide across the floor, fighting now for wind, for that leverage that would allow him to roll out from under the man and break free. His fingers touched the gun belt, lying partly under the cot, and a surge of hope rocked through him. He gathered the belt in a tight grip and lashed out at the indistinct shape looming over him.

He heard the dull, chinking sound the heavy buckle made as it struck Halverson's head. The fingers at his throat relaxed and dropped away. The dark shape over him sagged. Ryan, gasping for breath, shoved with his last remaining strength, and Halverson tipped stiffly sideways and went out of his line of vision, thudding softly to the floor.

Ryan crawled across the room to where the gun lay, his head clearing with each deep draught of air. He retrieved the holster and strapped the belt back on, dropping Halverson's gun into place. He moved slowly and painfully to the man's side and peered closely at him in the dimness. The raw imprint of the buckle's edge was a livid mark across his temple.

Ryan felt for his pulse.

The man was not dead, but he likely would be quiet for some time.

Wasting no more time, he moved to the door and moved stealthily into the open. Rain drove into his face, and he took a moment to get Halverson's hat. His own was gone, lost somewhere after Turk Paulson had knocked him out the night before.

There was dim light burning in the kitchen at the main house, and, watching it intently for a moment or two, he saw the dumpy figure of the cook pass before the window and back again, doing his chores. Either he had not heard the explosion of Halverson's gun or else just assumed it to be a clap of thunder. Keeping close to the fence, he limped to the barn and entered. He again hesitated, certain that no one was in the huge, gloomy building, but taking no chances. Satisfied after a minute's listening, he passed along the stalls until, at last, he came to the roan. He heaved a sigh. The blue was still saddled, only the bridle having been removed to make it easier for him to eat.

Ryan had him ready in a short time. He mounted up in the stable, taking a moment to check the caliber of Halverson's gun. It was the same common size as his own, and for this he was grateful. He refilled the spent cartridge from his belt and rode out into the yard.

Rain was coming down much harder. Pools were beginning to form in the yard, making dark mirrors in the night. He started for the road, when a flash of lightning brought everything into quick, brilliant relief. Two figures stood near the kitchen door: Halverson, weaving uncertainly on his feet, and the cook, an old double-barreled shotgun clutched in his hands. While Ryan had been bridling the roan, Halverson had revived sufficiently, at least, to make his way to the kitchen and summon the cook.

Ryan drew his gun and laid a shot at their feet. Halverson staggered back and fell against the side of the house, mud and water splattering over him. The cook yelled, and the shotgun boomed into the darkness, lead pellets whistling off, high overhead. Ryan touched the roan with his spurs, and they raced toward the pair. When he drew abreast, he snapped another bullet toward them, digging more mud from beneath their feet. The cook dropped his gun and ducked inside the kitchen door. Halverson sat weakly back, his mouth working with curses.

That would hold them. Ryan swung the roan due south toward the Strickland place.

# Chapter Eighteen

The roan's pace was a fast and reckless one. The going was slippery over the wet prairie and through the draws, and Ryan knew he was taking short odds on the blue's falling. But he had to reach Strickland's; he had to get there as soon as possible. He realized he could not overtake Hugh Baldwin and his crew, but, with a little good luck, he might arrive before they had done much damage.

Rain was a steady punishment upon his face and neck, the cold drops sharp and stinging when they struck. Lightning flashed regularly, broad sheets that flooded the landscape with blue-white brilliance. Some of the draws were beginning to run with foaming brown water rushing downhill. By morning the creek would be glutted and out of its low banks. It was one of those rare, hard rains that came to the Vega country, often doing far more damage than good.

He came into the S-Bar property at the far, northwest corner. The roan was breathing heavily from his labors, but he had stayed upright, slipping only once or twice on the long run and never entirely going to his knees. Ryan kept him pointed due south until he was parallel with the tamarisk windbreak, and then cut back eastward. He thus approached the buildings of the Strickland spread from the blind side, and, therefore, could not be so readily seen by any of Hugh Baldwin's crew that were on guard. That seemed unlikely to Ryan, however. Baldwin had little fear of intervention from any quarter, particularly where Ryan was concerned. Indeed, Baldwin had reached a point where, in the overwhelming certainty of his own power, he frankly ignored all possibilities of danger.

There was no light in the front of the house, when Ryan halted the roan in the depths of the tamarisks. The thick growth was some protection from the drizzle, and, after he had stepped from the saddle, he stood for a time, listening and considering his best move. The S-Bar lay in deep quiet, only the steady rain setting up a drumming noise. Under the vivid flashes of lightning he could see the wet, glistening buildings silhouetted against the sky, its few trees and fences. The pools of water deepened in the low places of the yard, reflecting these trees and fences.

He wondered if he could have overtaken and passed Hugh Baldwin, if they could have stopped, waiting for the rain to let up, before they moved in on the S-Bar. But where would they hole up? There was no place between unless they chose to swing far westward where there was one of the line shacks. That didn't sound like an idea Baldwin would have. He was not the sort to countenance any delays once he had gotten under way. Too, he doubted if he had overtaken them. With the start they had, even before he had tangled with Halverson, it would have been a near impossibility. No, they were there, hiding probably in one of the structures on the place, preparing to strike.

Ryan left the roan and crossed the porch of the main house. The door was closed but not locked, just as he had found it previously. He pushed it open softly and stepped inside. There was a low drone of voices coming from the kitchen, and he paused, trying to isolate and identify them. It was possible Baldwin was there, endeavoring to swing Ann Strickland to his way of thinking. But if he was, Ryan could not distinguish Baldwin's deep tones.

It was difficult to tell who it was. The rain maintained its steady rattle on the roof and against the glass of the windows. He listened intently and came finally to the conclusion that it was only two people, Ann and someone else—George Cobb, perhaps, or it could be some neighbor come to pay his condolences for the death of Tom Strickland. But it was more logical to believe it was the S-Bar foreman. Ryan moved silently across the room, opened the connecting door, and stepped into the kitchen.

George Cobb sat at the table, his back to Ryan. Ann, standing near the big range, was in the act of pouring each a cup of coffee. When Ryan came into the room, she lifted her glance to him, and he saw her eyes spread wide into circles of surprise.

"You!"

George Cobb came around in his chair. His dark brows snapped down into an angry line, and he clawed at the gun at his side.

Ryan said—"Don't do it!"—in a sharp, crackling sort of way.

His hand had dropped to where it hovered lightly over the curving handle of his pistol. His face had a cold, empty sort of look. Cobb relaxed gently, letting his arms fall slowly forward.

Ryan said: "I've got no quarrel with you, George. Let's don't begin one now."

Ann Strickland met his gaze. "Who is your quarrel with, Jim?"

"Nobody in here," Ryan answered. Then: "Baldwin been here since dark?"

He was wet to the skin. Water dripped from his soaked clothing and was forming small puddles on the floor around him. He removed his hat—Halverson's hat—and held it at his side.

"Not tonight," Cobb said. "Why?"

"I'm looking for him," Ryan answered.

Cobb laughed. "Not the way we heard it. Understand Meldrum's posse had orders to shoot you on sight. Since you murdered Frank Sears, you got a right big price on your head."

Ryan heard the words and felt their shocking impact. This was more of Hugh Baldwin's work. He should have expected it. He should have known the cattleman would pass a tale such as that on to the marshal. "So, I murdered Frank Sears. Is that what you've been told?"

"That's what they say. You shot him down when he flat quit your outfit. He wouldn't go along with what you're doin', and you nailed him to keep him from talkin'."

"This was Hugh Baldwin telling you all this?"

Cobb nodded. "He was by here, lookin' for the marshal. You sayin' it ain't so? That Frank ain't dead?"

"Frank's dead," Ryan replied, "but not by my gun. Two of Baldwin's crew did it."

Cobb shrugged his thin shoulders. "Seems to me like you always got a different story than everybody else. They're always wrong, but you're always right, to hear you tell it."

"That's exactly right," Ryan said in a close, tight voice. "Everybody else is wrong. I'm telling you that straight, and you'd better start believing me if you expect to come out of this mess with a whole skin."

Ann Strickland, quiet during this interchange between Ryan and the S-Bar foreman, suddenly spoke. "Believe you? What reason do any of us have for believing you? A gunman, a killer who thinks nothing of shooting a man down in cold blood! Why should anybody ever believe a man like you against one like Hugh Baldwin or the marshal? Or even Reno Davis? You can't deny any of what's been said about you."

Ryan met her gaze, seeing the uncertainty lying there in her eyes, the alarm and disturbance his presence in the room was creating. He shook his head in a weary fashion. "No, I'll not deny what has been said about my time with the gun. You've said some things that aren't true, but that's neither here nor there. The main thing is that you are dead wrong about Hugh Baldwin. And that's why I'm here now."

Rain battered against the walls of the house, and a rising wind rattled the windows and doors. Somewhere outside an unfastened gate slapped steadily against its post.

"This morning Baldwin and his crew burned down my place. He brought them here to do the same for you tonight."

George Cobb snorted. "That'll be a little hard to do in all this wet."

"It won't stop him," Ryan answered. "Not now."

Cobb paused, looking squarely at Ryan in a perplexed way. "Now, just why would Hugh want to do that? You give me one good reason."

"He was by here today, wasn't he? Wanted you to sell out?"

Ann said: "Yes, he was. But he's offered to do that before."

Ryan shook his head. "I can't make you people understand what you're up against. Hugh Baldwin is a dangerous man. He's out to take over this country, just like his pa tried to do years ago, even if it means wiping out every outfit in it. I've seen his kind before. Once they've had a taste of what force can do for them, they go wild. And Hugh's had his taste."

Cobb stirred in his chair. Ann glanced toward the rain-covered window. Cobb said: "You don't make much sense, mister. If Hugh's gone loco like you say, why would he be blamin' it on you? You're a newcomer to this country.

There's a dozen others he could have pointed to."

"It's you that's not making sense. Being a newcomer made me the best bet. And I happened to be handy that day Tom Strickland was shot. Now, if he burns down this place tonight, I'll get the credit for it just like I did for the bullets that went into Frank Sears's back."

"You sure wouldn't be burnin' down your own place," Cobb admitted thoughtfully.

Ryan shook his head. "I don't know how Baldwin will explain that," Ryan said then. "Unless he gives them a yarn that he did it so I'd have no place to headquarter from. It would be a thin story, but people would believe Hugh. They have so far," he added with a lot of bitterness, looking at Ann.

She said: "You told me you were leaving here. What made you come back?"

Ryan shrugged. "I don't know for sure." Purpose and cause were all confused in his mind: Ann, or Frank Sears, or the thought of a man like Hugh Baldwin running loose and roughshod over the land. He could not separate any of the reasons; they all seemed to interlock and hinge, one upon the other. He said: "Finding Frank Sears there, shot in the back, I suppose. He was a fine old man who never hurt anyone. I guess that's my reason. Anyway, it will do."

"I see," Ann murmured in an odd, falling voice.

"Still don't any of it make much sense to me," Cobb growled. "I've known Hugh a right smart of time. He's tough, and I reckon he keeps what's his, but I don't see him pullin' all these things you've been talkin' about. Sure, we've had trouble with Hugh, but that's to be expected. Everybody has some trouble, now and then. Seems like nowadays you can hardly move without rilin' some jasper. Nope, Ryan, I just can't swallow your tale, not after considerin' your reputation as a gunman and killer."

Anger brushed swiftly through Jim Ryan. "You keep mentioning the past. Now, I want to tell you something. If it was just you and the S-Bar alone in this, I'd forget about it and walk out that door. I'd leave you to Hugh Baldwin and his Circle X crowd. But there's others involved. He gets my place, then the S-Bar. Next time it will be some other rancher or homesteader. Nothing's going to stop him if we don't stand together and fight him. If you can't see it that way, then it will be me and my gun alone, but I'll not quit now."

"That's your answer to all things," Ann broke in quietly. "Always a gun . . . a bullet."

Ryan shook his head. "No, I would not say that is true."

"How can taking a life be right? It's wrong to kill a man . . . any man."

Ryan stared at the woman in surprise. She had just lost her father to a bullet fired by a hired gunman—how could she feel that way?

"A man does what he thinks is right when he's dealing with the likes of Reno or Baldwin . . . others like them . . . like Thompson and Santee," he added. He'd not leave the Stonebreaker's Ridge country until he'd squared up with them. He owed Frank Sears that much. "Time comes," he continued, "when you fight fire with fire. Men like Hugh Baldwin follow no rule books. You handle them as they figure to handle you."

Cobb said: "What made you think Hugh was comin' here tonight?"

"I was there, at Circle X. They had me penned up with a guard, a man named Halverson. I overheard Reno telling him they were coming here. Later I got away and followed."

"Baldwin caught you, eh? Why didn't he turn you over to Ross? Him and that posse's still huntin' in the hills."

Ryan remembered Baldwin's instructions to the men who

worked with the posse: keep the marshal busy, keep him working the hills and out of the way for a couple more days. He repeated this to Ann and George Cobb.

The old foreman stroked his chin. "Makes some sense . . . part of it," he admitted. "Some don't. But there could be a reason for it. I just can't figure Hugh would do a thing like that and. . . ."

Ryan's patience finally snapped. "All right," he barked, "have it your own way! Believe what you want . . . believe Baldwin or Reno Davis or anybody else! I'll handle this alone, in my own way, and if you get hurt in the doing of it, remember it was of your own making."

He wheeled to go back through the living room. Halfway across the parlor he pulled up short. Ann's stricken voice had cried out: "Look! Fire in the barn!"

# Chapter Nineteen

Ryan spun around, pain from his injured leg jabbing through him. George Cobb came off his chair in a long leap and wrenched open the door. Rain was still falling in a steady sheet and thunder pulsed a low crescendo through the blackness. Through the barn doors and the loft windows Ryan could see the bright flare of reaching flames as they raced through the interior of the structure.

Cobb yelled: "I'll get out the crew! Got to get the stock out of there!"

Ryan jumped to intercept the foreman, but Cobb was outside and running hard for the bunkhouse. Sudden lightning shattered the blackness. Ryan saw the shape of Reno Davis astride his horse, waiting somewhere near the center of the yard. Davis's gun roared as the lightning died. In the succeeding flash, a split second later, George Cobb was a writhing, long shape in the mud. A small cry escaped Ann Strickland's lips.

"Douse that lamp!" Ryan ordered, and dropped to his knees. Gun in hand, he crawled his way to the still open doorway.

The room plunged at once into darkness. Ryan waited for the next eerie spread of light, the spot where Reno Davis had been, fixed in his mind. The shot had roused the crew, and the windows of the bunkhouse were now yellow squares. The door flung back, and a man, clad only in his underwear, stood framed there. The vicious attack of a gun, coming from over near the flaming barn, drove him stumbling back inside. Im-

138

mediately the bunkhouse lamp went out. Lightning came again, but Davis was no longer in sight. There was only the crumpled shape of George Cobb, lying down in the shallow pool.

"There a rifle in here?" Ryan asked in a low voice.

Ann said: "Yes. Mine."

"Get it. Stay in here where you can watch the yard. Shoot anybody that tries to get close to the house. *Anybody* . . . understand?"

"Yes," Ann replied in a small voice.

He heard her moving about the room. "Better lock that front door," he said, remembering he had twice found it open.

In a few minutes she was back. He caught the faint shine of light on the rifle metal. "Now, remember, shoot first and we'll look afterwards. Don't trust anybody."

"Except you," she said. "I know that now, Jim."

His tone relented a little. "Sometimes things are hard to believe. The people you least suspect are your worst enemies. Are you all set?"

"Yes. What are you going to do?"

"Go out there. I want to look at George. He might still be alive. And I want to get your crew together and see if we can stop Baldwin before this gets worse."

Gunshots suddenly began to racket near the barn, the reports mixing with the screaming of the trapped horses. Despite the rain's steady fall, the fire was beginning to push through the building to the outside. New flames were darting within several of the smaller sheds where Baldwin's men had thrown torches. Lightning ripped the night again and again, and Ryan, crouched within the doorway, saw the bunkhouse was deserted. Ann's crew was out there somewhere in the yard, starting to fight back. This at once created a new problem for him: they could easily mistake him for Circle X. But he would have to take that chance.

Ryan moved to leave, keeping well down. He felt Ann's fingers touch him lightly. She said: "Be careful, Jim. After this night I'll have nothing, only you."

Ryan made no reply for a long moment, considering her words. He said then—"I'll be back, don't worry."—and darted out into the sopping darkness.

He moved quickly away from the doorway, staying as close as possible to the house itself so as to offer very little target to any Circle X man. Reaching the corner of the building, he lay full-length in the mud and water, waiting to cross the open yard to the corral. Getting set, still favoring the bad leg, he crouched. It was cold, bitterly cold in the rain, but this, like the restricting leg, he tried to ignore. He wanted only to meet with Reno Davis and Hugh Baldwin. And after them would come the two who had cut down Frank Sears.

Lightning came, a great, blinding sheet that lit up the yard in bluish-white brightness. It held for a long moment and closed off. Ryan, taking a deep breath, leaped to his feet and sprinted across the open ground. He came dangerously near to falling when his feet skidded on the slick mud, but he caught himself and finally reached the corral fence. No shots came lacing through the night after him, and he concluded he had not been seen. Keeping low again, he trotted along the fence until he was but a few feet from Cobb's prostrate form. Lightning flashed, and he had his full look at the foreman and knew at once he was dead. Davis's bullet had struck him squarely in the forehead. Likely he went down without ever knowing what had happened.

Ryan moved on toward the bunkhouse. The shooting had almost ceased. Only a report coming, now and then, when a man saw movement he knew was not a friend. Ryan could hear the crackling of flames rising above the drumming raindrops. The horses had stopped their screaming, all dead by this time. Ryan waited, his eyes probing the darkness ahead. In the next quick explosion of light he saw a man crouched behind one of the feed wagons, his face turned toward the barn.

Ryan crept in close. "Don't shoot. I'm behind you."

"Who is it?"

"Ryan. Where's the rest of the crew?"

Surprise rode the man's tone. "Ryan? Whose side you on? Who's that out there?"

"Baldwin and his crowd . . . Circle X."

There was silence for a moment. "I thought I saw Reno Davis out there. By God! Only today they was here, makin' out like they was our best friends. They get George?"

"Straight through the head. Reno got him when he started across the yard after you and the rest of the men."

"Reno," the 'puncher murmured in a low, remembering sort of way. "Ain't he the one you claimed killed old Tom?"

Ryan answered: "Yes. Couldn't have been anybody else."

Several shots broke out then in that area between the barn and the feed house. Ryan got to his feet. "Looks like that's where we ought to be."

"Let's go," the 'puncher said, and started along the scatter of discarded wheels, crippled, unused vehicles, and other old equipment strung along the bunkhouse. They picked up another S-Bar man, and the three of them reached the wagon shed just as a flash of lightning silhouetted a man riding across the yard. It was Hugh Baldwin.

"My meat," the first 'puncher declared, and slammed a quick shot at the cattleman.

Ryan said quickly—"Scatter!"—and lunged away.

Immediately a dozen bullets laced the spot where they had

crouched. Ryan pulled up against the overturned bed of a wagon. "All right?" he called softly.

"All right," a voice came back.

"Me, too," came the other. "By jeemies, that was close! You hit Baldwin, Tod?"

"Don't know. Too dark to see much."

Ryan took advantage of the following lull to cross the calf yard and work in closer to the barn. The far side of the doomed building was visible to him from there, and, when the next flash of light blanketed the place, he saw Baldwin for the second time, along with several of his crew. They were milling about, glistening yellow shapes in the lurid glow. The fire within the barn was beginning to die down, only the soaked outer shell remaining upright. Most of the roof was gone in spite of the rain.

"Get up there and get a fire going in the main house!" Baldwin's voice shouted.

"How about the girl? She's still in there, ain't she?"

"She'll come out, once you get a blaze going!" Baldwin yelled back. "Rest of you boys, work on those sheds. And that feed house. I don't want anything left here but ashes when we're through."

"Somebody over there, hiding along the bunkhouse," a voice spoke up. "Watch it."

Ryan strained his eyes to locate the man delegated the job of firing the main house. But in the blackness he could pick out no movements. And the noise of the rain and hissing of embers drowned out all sound. He waited tensely for a flash of lightning. It came suddenly. Immediately he heard the crack of Ann's rifle, twice in rapid succession.

In a moment the Circle X rider was back, coming into the pale flare of light behind the barn. Ryan heard him swear and say: "Can't get close enough. She's got a rifle there, just

142

waitin' for a man to come up."

Reno Davis's voice called across the yard—"I'll take care of it, Hugh."—in his drawling, confident way.

Ryan came quickly to his feet and hurried toward the house. He was gambling on the lightning—or the darkness again, that there would be no revealing flash until he reached a point where he could intercept Davis. Luck was with him. He reached that point and waited, hearing the man coming. The horse was walking slowly through the puddles and deeper pools, its hoofs making wet, mushy sounds in the mud.

Ryan remained silent until the horse was a short ten feet distant. Then: "Reno . . . right here."

Davis fired at the sound of Ryan's voice. But Ryan had spoken and stepped away. He fired then, aiming at the orange bloom of Davis's gun. He heard the bullet strike dully and drive the wind out of the man in a great explosion of breath. The horse shied away, slipping badly on the wet ground, and Davis came out of the saddle in a heap. Waiting patiently, Ryan saw him lying prone, face turned upward, when lightning came again.

Bedlam had broken out. A welter of shots crackled behind the barn. Baldwin's crew began to answer. A man shouted— "Hey, Reno!"—and then was drowned out by another flurry of gunshots.

Ryan, keeping close to the ground, doubled back. The Strickland crew had collected near the feed house and were pouring a merciless fire into Baldwin's men. Ryan stumbled over a dead body and fell flat. In the next break of light he saw Baldwin and three or four of his riders, lined up in an irregular sort of formation, returning the fire. He recognized the huge bulk of Turk Paulson, down to his knees, hat gone, sinking slowly to the sodden ground as a half dozen bullets caught up with him.

He laid his own shots at Baldwin, thus placing the cattleman and his crew in a wicked cross fire. A yell went up at once. A horse screamed in agony, and another voice cried out: "They got some help!"

Ryan ran to the corner of the barn that was still hissing loudly as cold water continued to fall upon glowing embers. In the uncertain, dim light of one of the sheds, he could vaguely see Baldwin and the men who were still mounted. Two of them wheeled suddenly and charged off into the night. Another, close by Baldwin, sagged as a bullet struck him, and slid from the saddle.

"Hugh!" Ryan sent his call out through the rain-soaked darkness and stepped away from the barn.

Baldwin fired wildly and spurred his horse away, beyond the pale flare of flames. Ryan withheld his shot, trying for a better position from which to shoot. A Circle X rider crossed in front of him, his face white and glistening from the rain. He threw a glance at Ryan, visibly startled by what he saw. He snapped a hurried shot, but it was yards wide. Ryan laid his answer through the darkness and had an indefinite vision of the man reeling and grabbing at his shoulder, and then fading from sight.

At the end of the barn Ryan hesitated, standing as close to it as the heat from the smoldering wood allowed. He was watching that point of darkness into which Baldwin had plunged. He knew the cattleman would not be there now, that he likely would appear some distance away. But the flash of lightning might catch him, still moving. The broad sheet of light came and held a long while as it flickered strongly. The yard and its surroundings came out sharply: the huddled shape of Turk Paulson and two others, a downed horse. But Baldwin was not to be seen.

"S-Bar!" Ryan called.

Strickland's crew came from their various points. Four men. They gathered soberly around him. The 'puncher, Tod, whom he had first met near the bunkhouse, was not among them.

Ryan said: "Any of you see where Baldwin went?"

There was a murmur of noes. One said: "I saw him take a shot . . . at you, I reckon . . . and then dive back out of sight. Ain't seen him since."

Baldwin had got away. Seeing his crew melt before his eyes, he had turned tail and fled, fearing the death he so ruthlessly meted out to others.

"You men clean up this mess as best you can," Ryan said then. "Do it now, before daylight. Get George Cobb's body and these others out of the yard before Ann sees them. One of you better start out and find the marshal."

"Where you goin'?"

"After Baldwin," Ryan said. "This thing's not finished until we get him."

"I'm goin' with you," one of the cowpunchers said at once.

Ryan said—"No."—in a short, terse way. "I'll take care of Baldwin."

# Chapter Twenty

Ryan swung away from the men and struck out across the yard, heading for the windbreak and the roan. He stayed purposely clear of the house. Knowing Ann was safe and that he had little time if Baldwin had it in mind to leave, he wanted to lose as few minutes as possible. But she saw him and came out into the open.

"Is it all over?"

"All done here," he replied, halting in stride. He bent his steps to hers.

"Was it so very bad?"

"Pretty bad," he said, not wanting to go into any details. He was remembering the things she had said about guns and the horror and death that rode with them.

"Did . . . was Hugh . . . ?" she began haltingly.

Ryan shook his head. In the darkness he could not see her face clearly, but she was standing close. "No, he ran when he saw his outfit going down or deserting . . . Reno and Turk Paulson and a couple others are down. I'm going after Baldwin now. I'll find him at his place, I expect, getting ready to leave the country."

"Can't you let him go? Do you have to go after him?" she asked at once. "Why does it have to be you? It's Meldrum's job now."

"No time to wait for the marshal," Ryan explained patiently. "He could be in the next territory by the time we located Meldrum and convinced him that Baldwin was at the bottom of all this trouble. It's something I have to do myself, anyway, Ann. A personal matter."

"Yes," she replied in a heavy voice, "I suppose that's the way it is."

"The rain's beginning to let up," Ryan said. "You better get inside and get on some dry clothing. Then I want you to go into town. Get away from here until the crew gets things cleaned up. This is no place for you."

"Why not? It's my home, my ranch. Why shouldn't I stay here? You think I'm afraid of . . . of death out here?"

"No," Ryan said, "I don't think that. But this isn't over yet. Trouble could come again. I want you to tell me you will do as I say . . . that you'll go into town and stay there."

"All right," she agreed in that same lost tone. "Will you come? Will I see you later?"

He nodded. "Before I leave."

"You're going on when this is over?"

He said simply—"Yes."—and turned then to go.

Before he had taken a full step, she had moved in close to him. She threw her arms around his neck and placed a kiss, warm and soft, upon his lips.

"For everything, I'm sorry," she said. "Can you ever forgive me for not trusting you? For the terrible things I have said?"

He pulled slowly away, taking her by the shoulders. He said gently: "Think no more about it, Ann. Truth is a hard thing to recognize at times. As for mistakes, I've made my share of them."

"But can you forget it? That's important, Jim. Can you forget the things I've said and done?"

Ryan said honestly: "I'm glad to be alive. Grateful for that, I'll question nothing else."

She pulled away from him, and he knew she was finding no satisfaction in his words. But he could see no other way to say it. He knew now what lay ahead, for he was a marked man and the future was an uncertain, indefinite path. The dark shadows of the past were not dead. They were here, this night, and the search would begin again, as before.

"Be careful," she said, turning toward the door. "If not for my sake, for your own."

He waited until she had entered the doorway, her slim shape vague in the gloom, and then wheeled away to the roan. For the first time since the fight had begun, he was conscious of the dull and familiar throb in his leg, but it bothered him only a little now. He drew the blue into the open and stepped to the saddle. It was cold, soaked wet, and not at all comfortable, but he was drenched to the skin anyway, and after a few seconds it was not noticeable.

He cut back through the tamarisks, following as direct a route as he could find. The rain had settled into a fine, cloudy mist, and in the east the clouds were breaking up, preparing for a dawn not far away.

When they broke into the open country, the roan swung into a long and easy lope. Pools of water splashed beneath him, and he slid once, coming into a long-sloped draw, but he managed to stay up. Ryan did not press the big horse hard but let him choose his own pace and his own trail, and in that manner they soon were crossing the south pasture of the Circle X holdings. Unsure as to how many of the crew might still be around, Ryan swung west and approached the buildings from the spring, just as he had done the previous night.

Five horses—Baldwin's and four others—stood at the rail. Ryan studied them for a time, recognizing them finally as those used by the riders sent to work with Ross Meldrum. All, apparently, were gathered in the front room of Baldwin's house, holding a council of war or being paid off by the cattleman. While Ryan pondered his best move, the four men came out, mounted up, and rode off toward the north. They soon were out of sight, showing no indications of stopping, and Ryan concluded that, like rats leaving the doomed ship, they were getting out while there was still time.

He brought the roan in, moving alongside the house, slipping quietly from the saddle when he reached the building's corner. Anchoring the blue, he drifted softly across the porch and reached for the door handle.

Baldwin's voice said: "Come in, Ryan."

Ryan halted, momentarily caught off balance, but his gun flew into his palm at the cattleman's first word. Alert for some trick, he opened the door and stepped inside. In the center of the room Hugh Baldwin faced him. He looked much older, somehow, and very tired and worn, and his eyes had a dull, empty cast.

"It took you a long time to get here."

Ryan watched the cattleman closely, still wary despite the man's unarmed condition and beaten manner. This was too easy; this was not the way he had anticipated Hugh Baldwin would wind things up. "I was delayed a few minutes," he answered slowly. "Why, you in a hurry?"

"Not any more," Baldwin said wearily. "It's all down a hole now. You saw the last of a damned fine spread ride out of here five minutes ago, paid off and heading for new country. The whole works . . . the ranch, Pike, Reno Davis, and all the rest . . . are gone. Either dead or skipping the country for fear of their necks. I'm the last of Circle X, Ryan."

"Man pays for his mistakes," Ryan said softly. "It's an old rule."

Keeping a narrow gaze upon the cattleman, he was beginning to wonder if the man wasn't really sincere, after all. It looked and it sounded genuine, yet Ryan was not fully convinced.

"Man starts out to do something, to build to the limit. He should get there. But something went wrong . . . just what, I don't know."

"You know, Hugh," Ryan corrected dryly, "nobody knows that better than you. Every time you stepped on a little man, you knew exactly what was going on. Nobody ever built much on that kind of a foundation. And you knew that was a fact, too."

"I suppose so," Baldwin murmured. "But, sometimes, a man gets to moving so fast, he can't see what's going by him. Well, what comes now?"

"We're going to town, like we started to do last night. I want a few things straightened up, including my name. I want that cleared with Meldrum and everybody around here. You're the one man left that can do that."

"Your name cleared?" Baldwin echoed with a half smile. "Since when did you get so touchy about your name? Pike told me all about you, Ryan, that night in the saloon. I know who you are and what you are, and everything about you."

"That was a long time back," Ryan said in a soft voice. "No point in bringing it up in this case. It has nothing to do with it. Leave it in the past."

"You figure maybe the girl won't like it, eh?"

Ryan shrugged. "I hardly think that matters . . . one way or another. By tomorrow I'll be out of this country."

Baldwin shook his head. "Maybe so, but I've got a little news for you. You'll have to leave without this business of having your name cleared, as you call it. I'm not going back with you, Ryan. I know where I stand, and I'm smart enough to know what my chances are when all this gets out. I let you walk in here, Ryan, because that's the way I wanted it. I could have thrown a gun down on you while you were coming up from the spring. I saw you cross and turn and come up the fence, and I watched you get off that roan horse. Now, we'll have it out, man to man. I figure I haven't got a show against a man of your kind when it comes to guns, but it will beat a rope and a bunch of gawking sodbusters watching me swing."

Ryan thought for a moment. "If all that's true, why didn't you leave with the others? Why didn't you head north with them?"

"Turn tail and run with them?" Baldwin shook his head as if that had not occurred to him before. "I can't answer that except maybe to say I hadn't thought of it and wouldn't have done it, if I had. Maybe this is a little hard for you to understand, but I couldn't do it. Call it pride or bullheadedness or foolishness . . . I don't care which. Whatever it is, I just couldn't do it. That make any sense to you?"

Ryan nodded. He knew what it was—that fierce pride that rules a man and will not let him break even when necessary. And Baldwin could never drop down to a level with the men he had worked, had driven so arrogantly. "I understand all right, Hugh. But we aren't going to play this your way. I won't draw on you."

"Then you'll be a dead hero. Either I go out of here feet first, or you do. Take your choice."

Ryan stared at Baldwin.

The cattleman smiled back. "You think I'm afraid of a bullet . . . of dying?"

"Then why did you run out at Strickland's?"

Baldwin shrugged. "This will make you laugh, Ryan. And laugh good. But I wanted one more look at my place before I was through. That funny to you?"

"No," Ryan answered quietly, thinking of his own desolate Box K. "It's not funny, Hugh. Not at all."

He moved suddenly across the room, his gun pressing at Baldwin. He flipped the cattleman's weapon into the corner.

A long, gusty sigh passed the man's lips. "Hell, Ryan, it's the only favor I ever asked of any man. Give me back my gun and let me try. Give me that much."

Ryan said curtly: "Forget it, Hugh. It's not my choice to make. Maybe I would welcome the chance to settle with you for Strickland and Frank Sears and a few others. But it can't be handled that way. This goes further than my own personal satisfaction."

From the doorway behind him, Ryan caught the faintest scrape of rough clothing against wood. In that same breath of time a voice barked: "Ryan! We're behind you! Drop that gun!"

He saw the smile break across Baldwin's face and a sly gleam come into his eyes. "By heaven, Marshal, you got here just in time! That was a close one!"

"Raise your hands, Ryan!" Meldrum said. "Watch him, boys."

The lawman brushed past Ryan, and three or four posse members crowded into the room. The marshal faced Ryan. He pulled the gun from his hand and stuffed it into his waistband. "You gave us a hard time of it," he said, "but I knew we'd catch up with you sooner or later."

Ryan said: "You're making a mistake. Baldwin's the man you want."

"Me?" Baldwin shouted. He laughed. "I was about to take you in when you got the drop on me. Never was much good with a gun. He's a slick one, Ross. Keep a sharp watch on him."

Ryan faced the marshal again. "You haven't been by the Strickland place?"

"No," Meldrum replied, "and I don't reckon we'd better, not while you're along. Old George Cobb's riled up enough at you to take you apart with his own hands. I expect he'd organize that crew of his into a necktie party if they could lay hold of you. I only got four men left, and we sure couldn't hold that bunch off for long once they made up their minds. Where's your crew, Hugh? Didn't see any of them around when we came in."

"What's not out hunting Ryan . . . are working stock. Been pretty short-handed with all this going on, and a man's got to keep his business running."

Ryan shrugged. Meldrum would believe anything Hugh Baldwin told him. He did not know about the fight at the S-Bar; that was why he still thought Ryan was suspect. And Baldwin, seeing his opportunity, was playing it for all it was worth. But he determined to try again.

"Marshal, I tell you this is a mistake. Bring Baldwin into town with me. Don't let him stay here because he sure won't be here when you come back for him. And that's just what you will have to do when you get the straight of what happened last night, and before."

One of the posse members grunted in disgust. "Never did know one of these hardcases that didn't cry like a baby when he got caught. They're all alike. Big and mean until they get caught."

Baldwin said: "Tell you what, Ross. You take him on into town. I've got to wait here until some of the crew shows up so I can tell them the hunt's over and to get back to work. Then I'll ride in. Ryan wants me in town for some reason, and I'll be glad to come and tell what I know about him."

"Fair enough," Meldrum said. He turned to Ryan. "All right, let's go."

Another of the posse members had found the roan and brought him around to the front. Meldrum motioned Ryan into the saddle and then tied his hands to the horn. He swung up onto his own bay pony and rode in close.

"Hate to shoot that horse," he said, ducking his head at the blue. "But that's the first thing that'll happen if you try any bad moves."

Ryan said: "Marshal, for the last time, you're making a bad mistake. I was taking Baldwin in when you came up. He's the man you're after, and I can prove it if you'll give me the chance. Main thing is to not let him get away before I can do that. Either leave a guard here with him or make him come along now."

"Didn't you hear what he said?" Meldrum asked. "He said he'd be along later, and Baldwin's word is good enough for me. He says he'll do it, and he'll do it."

Ryan shrugged. "All right, Ross. We're doing it your way."

They swung out into the yard and took the road for Gunstock. Over his shoulder Ryan saw Hugh Baldwin, standing in the doorway of his house. He was smiling.

# Chapter Twenty-One

Ryan rode in tight-lipped silence. Ranged around him were the posse members and Ross Meldrum, forming a half circle. All were grim and haggard from the days and nights of searching, and he knew there was small hope of convincing them of the truth. But with each step he knew Hugh Baldwin was that much closer to escape. That was what the cattleman would do now. Ryan had unwittingly planted the idea, and this time the cattleman would not wait. He was still slightly doubtful of Baldwin's story and his explanation, but it was of no importance now. The breaks had been with the cattleman, and he would not again fail to use them. It was a long ride into town, and, by the time Meldrum learned the truth, he would be far away and beyond reach.

When they rode off the prairie and dropped into the valley where the creek cut its way, Ryan made a final try. They crossed the bridge, and at the turnoff for the Strickland's S-Bar he twisted half around in the saddle and said to Meldrum: "Marshal, I'll say this once more. This is a bad mistake, and you're making it. Take me to Strickland's, and I'll prove everything I've said."

One of the posse men threw him an angry glance. "Aw, quit cryin', Ryan. You're not getting out of this, and you can make up your mind to that."

Meldrum only wagged his head stubbornly and rode wearily on.

Ryan said: "We had a showdown at Strickland's last night. Baldwin's crowd and the S-Bar crew. George Cobb was killed along with Reno Davis and several others. You'll get that news when we reach town, I expect. But you can save time by cutting over to Strickland's from here."

"Sounds like it was a reg'lar war," one of the men observed. "How come we didn't hear no shootin'?"

"Why, don't you remember, Dave? There was a storm last night! Lots of thunder and lightnin'. That's how come we didn't hear any of it."

The man's obvious sarcasm brought a grin to Meldrum's face. But all he said was: "Keep going."

The sun was well out, when they wheeled into Gunstock's single street. At once a crowd began to gather, forming in small groups that drifted quickly to the jail where Meldrum led his prisoner and guards.

"Stay mounted," he said to Ryan.

Meldrum swung heavily down from his horse. He stepped upon the short, raised porch fronting the building and turned to the murmuring crowd. Two of the posse members followed, taking a stand behind him.

"If you folks are hatching up any ideas, forget them. This man is my prisoner, and I aim to keep him one. And alive. Move along now. I don't want trouble from any of you."

Ryan searched the fan of upturned faces for Ann, for any of the Strickland crew. She was not there, and he did not recognize any of the others. Apparently none of them had yet come into town.

"Just wastin' good time," a voice called from the crowd. "We know he shot old Tom and Frank Sears. What's the sense of waitin' for the circuit judge?"

"Sure, everybody knows he done it," another added.

Ryan shifted his gaze to Meldrum. The gathering was in an ugly mood, and he could feel the undercurrent of strong resentment throbbing through it. It would take very little to turn into a violent mob. The marshal waited in stony silence. The lines about his mouth were gashed deeply by exhaustion, and his eyes reflected his weariness. In a slow, distinct tone he said: "I want every man Jack of you off this street in two minutes. Two minutes! After that, I'll take a scatter-gun and run you off!"

He ducked his head at the posse members standing near him. They wheeled together into the jail and returned a moment later, each carrying a double-barreled shotgun.

Meldrum took one of the weapons and cocked the tall, rabbit-ear hammers. The sound cracked through the hush. He said: "One minute's already gone."

Immediately a low rumble of dissent went up, but the crowd began to break apart. One man in a far-reaching voice said—"Killer like him ain't entitled to no trial."—but the gathering continued to drift away under the marshal's steady, unrelenting gaze.

Meldrum waited until the street was clear. Then: "All right, Ryan. Get down."

Ryan moved his wrists, reminding the man he was still pinned to the saddle. He was thinking fast, seeking for an opportunity to escape and intercept Baldwin before it was too late. Otherwise, the Vega could forget the cattleman. As far as he was concerned, he would be a free man before too many hours had passed. Ann, backed by the remainder of her crew, would substantiate his story and prove he was guiltless and in the right. Just as soon as she came into town that would happen. But, by then, Baldwin would be out of reach. Ross Meldrum would be responsible for the error, and the posse members would remember how Ryan had tried to persuade them all that they were making a mistake. But it would be too late then.

Somehow, Ryan could find no satisfaction in that realization. Men like Baldwin, who instigate trouble for their own advantage, had no right to freedom. They were like wild, roving dogs: if left to run free, they would soon infect the whole country and turn it into a hell for all decent people. And then there was the personal matter of Tom Strickland and Frank Sears. For Ann's sake, he wanted Baldwin held accountable for the death of her father. For his own, he wanted him brought to justice for Sears's death.

"Cut him loose, Dave," Meldrum ordered.

The man came off the porch, producing a jackknife from his pocket. He sliced through the light rope binding Ryan's wrists and stepped quickly back. Ryan swung down. As he came fully on his weak leg, it gave away, and he went onto the ground in a heap.

"Watch him!" Meldrum barked.

The man called Dave stared at Ryan's blood-stained britches and the bandage around his leg. "Reckon he's been shot, Ross. Got a lot of blood on him."

"Where'd you get that?" Meldrum demanded at once. "Why didn't you say anything about it, Ryan?"

Ryan shrugged. "You didn't give me much chance to say anything."

A buckboard wheeled into the far end of the street, and he threw a quick glance that way. But it was not Ann. Meldrum said: "Give Dave a hand there, Ritchie. I'll hold a gun on him while you get him inside."

Behind them, in the street, the two remaining posse members shifted on their horses. "You through with us, Ross?"

Meldrum said: "Reckon so, boys. Go on home and get some shut-eye. Thanks for the help."

Ryan heard them turn about and trot slowly away.

"You cost us all a lot of sleep," Meldrum observed. Then to his deputies: "Come on, come on, get him in a cell. I could sure use a little rest myself."

The two men helped Ryan to a standing position. One on each side, they assisted him into the small cubicle that served the marshal as both a jail and office.

"Think I ought to get the doc?" the man addressed as Dave asked when Ryan was settled on the cot.

Meldrum studied Ryan's injured leg for a moment. "Well, maybe you better."

Dave half turned, and Ryan, in one swift blow, jerked the pistol from the man's holster and came to his feet. He moved off, out of reach, to where he could cover all three men.

Sliding the gun gently back and forth over them, he said: "I don't like doing this, Marshal, but I like less the thought of Hugh Baldwin's getting away free. Now all of you get in that cell, turn your faces to the wall, and keep your hands high."

Meldrum swore under his breath in a steady stream. "I might have known this would happen."

Ryan tossed their guns onto Meldrum's desk, keeping only the one he had taken from Halverson. He slammed the cell door shut and put the keys with the guns.

"I'll be back," he said, "but likely there will be somebody along that will let you out before that."

"Where you headed?" Meldrum demanded.

Ryan gave him a short smile. "So you can follow me if you happened to get turned loose right away? Well, I guess it won't make too much difference in another thirty minutes. I'm going back to the Circle X . . . after Baldwin."

He swung about and walked onto the porch, closing the office door behind him. He climbed aboard the roan, looking neither right nor left, and cut the big blue around to the back of the jail. In this way he avoided the street, using instead the alleyway running behind the business buildings.

He kept the roan at a leisurely trot, not wanting to attract attention to his passage. But when he reached the edge of town, he touched the horse with spurs and headed for Baldwin's spread at a long, ground-consuming lope. Only one thing worried him at that moment: was he already too late?

Following earlier precautions, he again came to the ranch from the blind side. Leaving the roan well-hidden, and, remembering Baldwin's statement that he had watched him approach before, he came in from the opposite side of the structure. Stopping at the corner of the porch, he listened intently. Someone was inside. Whether it was Baldwin or not, he could not tell. It could be the cook or some other member of the crew collecting his belongings. He could hear the dry rattle of papers and the solid thud of a man walking about the room. Drawing his gun, he crossed the porch and, with one quick motion, jerked back the door.

Hugh Baldwin glanced up, startled. He was in the act of removing something from a lower drawer of his roll-top desk. Surprise flooded across his face. And then a slow, bitter smile cracked his heavy lips. He dropped whatever it was he had been holding and straightened up, keeping his hands open and well away from his sides.

He said: "You weren't gone long, Ryan."

"Not long," Ryan replied dryly. "And this time we'll go back together."

"I don't think so," Baldwin contradicted in the same dry way. "Look behind you, friend."

Ryan shook his head. "You know me better than that, Hugh. Nobody falls for that one."

Baldwin shrugged, the expression on his face having once again changed. "Speak up, Halverson . . . tell him how big the barrel of that gun you're pointing at his backbone is."

Halverson! Ryan had forgotten that man. He had dismissed him from his mind after the fight in the shed. And later, he had just assumed he had gone with the others. He must have been in the bunkhouse when he came up. Silently he cursed himself for his own carelessness.

"Drop that gun," Halverson ordered in a level voice. "And step away from it. Be my pleasure to split you down the middle with this Forty-Four."

Ryan kept his eyes on Baldwin's face. If he did as Halverson ordered, he would live—but not for long. They would see to it that he did not remain alive to do any talking. He weighed his chances on a sudden move, studying Baldwin's eyes. He came then to a cool decision. There was small chance of coming through these next few moments, no matter what he did.

Halverson murmured: "All right, Ryan. I'm telling you no more. Get those hands up . . . without that gun. Drop it!"

Ryan began to lift his arms, starting first at the elbows. His hands came away from his sides.

"Drop that gun!" Halverson barked in sudden alarm.

In that same fraction of time, Ryan spun away. He remembered this time to throw his weight to his good leg. He fired as he wheeled, ducking and lunging. It was point-blank range at Halverson. The room rocked with the explosion. Smoke boiled to the ceiling, and the acrid smell of gunpowder was strong. He saw Halverson stagger back, fall against the door, and go crashing through to the porch. Baldwin was then a blur, leaping for the opposite doorway, the one leading to the rear of the house.

"Hugh!" Ryan yelled his warning.

The cattleman did not pause. He was framed in the doorway when Ryan fired, aiming high. The bullet caught him in the shoulder and slammed him sideways with its force. Baldwin collided with something just outside the wall, a dresser, perhaps, or chest of drawers, and went down with a crash.

Outside, horses were pounding up. Ryan's mouth became a taut, grim line. Thompson and Santee? He'd settle with them next. A man's voice shouted something, but Ryan paid no heed. He crossed the smoke-filled room warily, gun still in hand, and looked upon the cattleman's sprawled body. Baldwin groaned.

"Get up, Hugh," Ryan said coldly. "You're a lucky man. You could be dead like Halverson."

From the floor Baldwin groaned again. "Better that I was," he said, and pulled to a sitting position.

Ross Meldrum's voice came from the porch, brisk and business-like. "I'll take care of him now, Ryan."

He pushed into the room. Ryan stepped away, seeing Ann Strickland standing out in the yard, waiting for him. Meldrum knew now. Ann had reached him and given him the story and the facts.

The marshal paused before Ryan. He had Hugh Baldwin on his feet and turned him over to a deputy. To Ryan he said: "Saying I'm sorry don't make for much, I guess. But a man gets off on the wrong track sometimes, and it's hard to straighten out. Hope you won't feel too hard about this. I hope you won't hold this against me."

Ryan shrugged. There was short patience in him for any man that relied purely on surface values, and never looked beneath the thin veneer all men wear. Too many good men were dead because of that very thing. But, already, this was the past.

"Forget it, Marshal," he said brusquely and, wheeling, stepped out into the open. Santee and Thompson were just moving away from the hitch rail after securing their horses.

"Santee! Thompson!" he called in a voice that could be

heard well down the street. "Frank Sears was a friend of mine. Try your gun on me."

A wildness possessed the shorter of the two. He came about, threw up both hands. "Weren't me that shot him down . . . was Thompson! I liked the old man, but Thompson here. . . ."

"That the way it was?" Ryan's question was hard as a blacksmith's anvil as he faced the taller of the pair. "Was it you that shot Sears in the back?"

Al Thompson settled himself in his boots. His ruddy face betrayed no emotion as his hands drifted slowly to his sides. He cast a contemptuous glance at Santee, turned his head slightly, and spat. "Yeah, reckon it was. You aim to do something about it?"

Anger stiffened Ryan. "You're a brave man . . . shooting him in the back."

Thompson's expression did not change. He nodded. "Hell, he had it coming . . . lying to me like he did."

The ranch yard was in dead silence. Meldrum muttered something in a protesting way but made no move. Two or three of the posse, yet to leave, watched from the shadowy depths of the room.

"Go for your gun," Ryan ordered quietly, "and keep looking at me. I want you to see the bullet coming."

Thompson swore. "Hell! This maybe ain't like the way. . . ."

"Can forget talking," Ryan cut in, "this is the time for settling up."

"No!" Ann Strickland's voice broke the tense hush as she hurried to Ryan. "Don't do it, Jim! Let the killing end here . . . for your sake . . . for mine."

Ryan hesitated, but his hard-surfaced eyes never left Al Thompson's coiled shape. His spread fingers hovering about the butt of the Forty-Five hanging on his hip remained motionless for a long breath and then relaxed slightly.

"She's right, son." Meldrum's voice was slow and careful. "Let your killing days end here and now."

Ryan shook his head. "I owe it to Frank Sears. Thompson shot him in the back. . . ."

"I know, and I'm agreeing that he's got to pay . . . but let it be at the end of a rope. You've got my word on that."

Ryan did not move for a time, and then his wide shoulders slowly went down.

"All right," he said softly. "Let it end here."

# Chapter Twenty-Two

They rode in silence, Ann Strickland on her little yellow pony, Ryan on the roan. Last night's rain was already disappearing under the drying rays of the sun, now a high, burning disc in a field of steel blue. They mounted a long, gentle knoll and, at the top, stopped. Here the trails forked, one for S-Bar, the other for Gunstock and the roads that radiated to the west, the south, or wherever a man was inclined to ride.

He was staring off into the distance, hazy and indeterminate beyond the green-gray of the prairies, and his thoughts were far-reaching and lonely.

She said then: "What will you do now?"

He did not turn his attention to her. "Anybody's guess. Another town, another place, I suppose. There'll be no more ranching. It's not for me. I know that now."

"Why not? You were doing fine. Why do you want to throw it all away?"

"Because there's nothing left here for me, Ann. I came into this country to settle down and forget the last five years of my life. In six months I am back where I started from." Abruptly he swung to her. "Even you reminded me of that."

"I know," she replied in a miserable voice. "I don't need you to tell me of it. It's something I won't soon forget."

He stirred in the saddle, solemn-faced and serious. "It's nothing now for you to remember. Truth is truth, no matter who it hurts. But it is a thing I had hoped to forget. I wanted that time to end when I lived by a gun, actually made my living with a gun. Ann, do you know what a bounty man is?

He is a gunman that goes after the outlaws other law officers leave alone. He goes after them for the reward their capture will bring. And he brings them in, dead or alive. I came here to forget that, to take over my pa's ranch and become a rancher. I thought I could, and I was on my way to that when Hugh Baldwin drew me into this trouble. I found then it is not possible for a man like me to become like any other."

The roan had moved slightly ahead of the pony, cropping at the sweet grass. Ann urged the calico forward until she was again next to him and could look into Ryan's set face. "And you think running away is the answer? That going to another town, even another world, will make it possible for you to forget your past?"

"It helps," he said.

"But that's all, and then for only a little while. The past is something none of us can escape, Jim. There's nothing any of us can do about it. It's not something we can just break off and throw away like the dead branch of a tree. You have to live with it, day by day, let it grow older until finally it isn't important any more."

He considered that for a long time, his eyes far off and deeply thoughtful. He said finally: "I never thought of it that way, but I guess that's the way it could be. A man should live down the things he wants to forget. I guess that's the only real answer." He shrugged. "I reckon I can try."

"And others forget sooner than you think."

He turned to her then, seeing her there beside him, so close, so desirable. "And you? Would you remember?"

"I would remember the good things," she replied at once, "and think of what would lie ahead for us."

He smiled. She was blushing for her own boldness. He reached over and laid his broad hand upon her own. "It will always be the good things for us," he said.

**Ray Hogan** is an author who has inspired a loyal following over the years since he published his first Western novel *Ex-marshal* in 1956. Hogan was born in Willow Springs, Missouri, where his father was town marshal. At five the Hogan family moved to Albuquerque where Ray Hogan still lives in the foothills of the Sandia and Manzano mountains. His father was on the Albuquerque police force and, in later years, owned the Overland Hotel. It was while listening to his father and other old-timers tell tales from the past that Ray was inspired to recast these tales in fiction. From the beginning he did exhaustive research into the history and the people of the Old West and the walls of his study are lined with various firearms, spurs, pictures, books, and memorabilia, about all of which he can talk in dramatic detail. Among his most popular works are the series of books about Shawn Starbuck, a searcher in a quest for a lost brother, who has a clear sense of right and wrong and who is willing to stand up and be counted when it is a question of fairness or justice. His other major series is about lawman John Rye whose reputation has earned him the sobriquet 'The Doomsday Marshal'. 'I've attempted to capture the courage and bravery of those men and women that lived out West and the dangers and problems they had to overcome,' Hogan once remarked. If his lawmen protagonists seem sometimes larger than life, it is because they are men of integrity, heroes who through grit of character and common sense are able to overcome the obstacles they encounter despite often overwhelming odds. This same grit of character can also be found in Hogan's heroines and, in *The Vengeance of Fortuna West*, Hogan wrote a gripping and totally believable account of a woman who takes up the badge and tracks the men who killed her lawman husband by ambush. No less intriguing in her way is Nellie Dupray, convicted of rustling in *The Glory Trail*. Above all, what is most impressive about Hogan's Western novels is the consistent quality with which each is crafted, the compelling depth of his characters, and his ability to juxtapose the complexities of human conflict into narratives always as intensely interesting as they are emotionally involving. His latest novel is *Soldier in Buckskin*.